K-PAX III

the worlds of prot
K-PAX III

gene brewer

BLOOMSBURY

First published in Great Britain 2002

Copyright © 2002 by Gene Brewer

The moral right of the author has been asserted

Bloomsbury Publishing Plc, 38 Soho Square, London W1D 3HB

A CIP catalogue record is available from the British Library

ISBN 0 7475 5783 7

10 9 8 7 6 5 4 3

Typeset by Palimpsest Book Production Limited,
Polmont, Stirlingshire

Printed in Great Britain by
Clays Ltd, St Ives Plc

For Karen

It often happens that the universal belief of one age—a belief from which no one was free or could be free without an extraordinary effort of genius or courage—becomes to a subsequent age so palpable an absurdity that the only difficulty is to imagine how such an idea could ever have appeared credible.

—John Stuart Mill

PROLOGUE

I N APRIL, 1990, I began the psychoanalysis of a 33-year-old mental patient who called himself "prot" (rhymes with "goat") and claimed to be from the planet "K-PAX."

I met with this young man on a regular basis for several months, during which time I was unable to shake his bizarre story and convince him of his earthly origins (he insisted he came here on a beam of light). The only useful information that emerged from these sessions was that he suffered from a severe sexual dysfunction, hated one or both of his parents, and took a dim view of human society in general.

However, after several weeks of analysis, it became clear that the patient was, in fact, suffering from a rare form of multiple personality disorder in which "prot" was a dominant secondary ego. The primary personality belonged to a man named Robert Porter, who had killed the murderer of his wife and nine-year-old daughter, and whose frustration, guilt, and grief had driven him to withdraw from the real world into an impenetrable shell guarded by his "alien" friend.

But prot, whatever his origin and nature, was a remarkable individual filled with arcane astronomical knowledge, a kind of genius savant. Indeed, he provided astronomers with valuable information on the planet K-PAX and others he claimed to have visited, as well as the double stars between which his world swung in a retrograde motion much like that of a pendulum.

Paradoxically, he seemed to possess a profound understanding of human suffering. Indeed, he was able, during his brief tenure at the Manhattan Psychiatric Institute, to hasten the recovery of a number of his fellow patients, some of whom had been with us for years. He even helped solve certain problems plaguing my own family!

Finally I managed, mainly through hypnosis, to break through Robert's carapace and make direct contact with his primary personality. For the first time, it seemed possible that I might be able to help him learn to deal with the death of his wife and daughter, and bring prot down to Earth.

The treatment, unfortunately, was interrupted by prot's announcement of his intention to return to his home planet on August 17, 1990, at precisely 3:31 A.M., a "journey" I was unable to persuade him to postpone. Faced with an impossible deadline, I tried to achieve an early resolution of Robert's crisis, which succeeded only in driving him deeper inside his protective shell. Moreover, the hospital was thrown into turmoil as many of the patients competed for a chance to go with him. Even some of the staff were lining up for the trip!

Robert declined to join him, however, and, when prot

"departed" at the scheduled time, was left behind in a state of intransigent catatonia. One of the other patients, a woman suffering from severe psychotic depression, did "disappear" along with prot, but what became of her and how she managed to leave the hospital is still a matter of conjecture.

The only bright spot in the episode was prot's promise to return to Earth in "approximately five of your years." And, true to his word, he returned precisely on August 17, 1995, to take over Robert's injured psyche once again and protect it from further harm.

This time prot refused to divulge the date of his next and, according to him, final departure and I had no idea how long I would have to work with Robert. But, this may have been something of a blessing in disguise: I could only assume there would be enough time to complete the protocol and, hopefully, to help Rob accept, at long last, what had happened to him and his family, and get on with his life.

Ironically, thanks in part to prot's cajoling, Robert now appeared ready and even willing to cooperate in his treatment program. As a result, it soon became evident that he had experienced a number of devastating incidents early in his life, including his sexual abuse at age five by a maternal uncle, and the death of his father when he was six. The loss of his only "friend and protector" (his father) was the last straw. It was then that he brought forth a new guardian (prot), who came from a faraway planet, one that was free from violence, cruelty, and loss, where all the events that had traumatized Robert's young life could never have happened.

Once these knots had been unraveled, and the existence of two additional alter egos revealed, it became possible, at last, for him to deal with his terrible past, including the death of his wife and daughter. Indeed, he made such rapid progress that he was discharged from MPI at the end of September, 1995, and moved in with his friend Giselle Griffin, a reporter who had been instrumental in discovering his true identity five years earlier (and subsequently became a kind of liaison between Robert and the outside world). It appeared that prot and the other two personalities, Harry and Paul, had become fully integrated into the psyche of Robert Porter, who seemed to have resumed a relatively normal life, i.e., there was no sign of a multiple personality disorder or any of the secondary symptoms (headaches, mental lapses, etc.) usually associated with this condition. For all practical purposes, Rob had been released from his psychological prison after more than thirty years of incarceration.

All of these events, including excerpts of my thirty-two sessions with Robert/prot, are described more fully in *K-PAX* and *K-PAX II*, which ended with the birth of his and Giselle's son Gene in the summer of 1997. At that time it appeared the family (including their Dalmatian, Oxeye Daisy) might, at last, live happily ever after.

Unfortunately, this turned out not to be the case.

SESSION THIRTY-THREE

T HE CALL came on Thursday, November 6, during my regular afternoon "Principles of Psychiatry" lecture at Columbia University, with which the Manhattan Psychiatric Institute is affiliated. Betty McAllister, our head nurse, contacted the chair of the psychiatry department there and insisted he interrupt my lecture to give me the bad news. Giselle had reported to Betty that prot had returned suddenly and without warning as Robert was bathing his son in their Greenwich Village apartment. Though somewhat dismayed, I wasn't entirely surprised by this unwelcome development. For one thing, multiple personality regression is not an uncommon occurrence and, for another, there were certain elements of Rob's rapid recovery in 1995 that had seemed almost too easy from the beginning—his seemingly well-rehearsed responses to certain questions put to him, for example.

It wasn't an emergency, however, and I decided to finish the lecture before returning to MPI. That was a mistake, and not the first of the long ordeal I was already dreading revisiting. I was so preoccupied with Robert's relapse that I became confused about some trivial point, much to the delight and even snickers of some of the medical students. Annoyed, I announced an immediate pop quiz; the derision turned to groans, and I left them with a question about Hessler's paradox, knowing full well there was no correct answer, requesting that a serious and (I assumed) trustworthy student collect the papers and forward them to me.

Prot and Giselle and their (Robert's) son were already waiting, with Betty, for me in my office when I returned to MPI. We greeted one another warmly. In the seven years I had known them, Giselle had become almost like a daughter to me, and prot, strange as it may seem, something of a trusted friend and advisor. He (like Rob, of course) was graying at the temples and sported a salt-and-pepper beard. I, on the other hand, had shaved mine off since our last meeting, retaining a trim mustache so as not to feel totally exposed.

He had lost none of his confidence and good cheer. Peering at me from behind his familiar dark glasses, he spouted, "Hiya, doc. Still beating your wife?" (This referred to an early session in which we were struggling to find a way to communicate with each other.)

Though I couldn't wait to interrogate prot, to find out where he had been while Robert lived his apparently normal life as a graduate student in biology at New York University, as well as devoted partner and father, I asked Betty to escort him to Ward Two while I spoke with Giselle. The prospect seemed to delight him, and he was off at once for the stairway to his former home, Betty hurrying along behind.

MPI is an experimental hospital which accepts only those

cases who have failed to make significant progress elsewhere. The different wards correspond to the floors on which they are located. Ward Two, for example, houses patients with various psychoses and severe neuroses. Those who make significant progress are eventually transferred down to Ward One, where they remain until they are ready to be discharged. The third floor is occupied by various sexual deviates, coprophiles, and others, as well as the autists and catatonics, and Ward Four by a number of psychopaths, those individuals who are a danger to both the staff and their fellow patients. The faculty and staff maintain offices and examining rooms on the fifth floor.

When prot and Betty had gone I closed the door, invited Giselle to sit down, and tweaked my namesake's little nose. He gurgled happily with an expression somewhere between prot's lopsided grin and Robert's shy smile. "Now," I said. "Tell me what happened."

Giselle looked worried, or perhaps merely frustrated, as people often are when they thought they had escaped from some skillet or other, only to find themselves dancing around an enormous frying pan. She gazed at me with her moist, doe-like eyes, which triggered in my mind vivid memories of our first encounter all those years ago when, curled up in that very chair, she had come to request permission to "roam the corridors" of MPI to research an article on mental illness for a national magazine.

"I don't know," she sighed. "One minute he was Robert, and the next he was prot." She snapped her fingers. "Just like that." The baby reached for her hand, apparently trying to understand where the "snap" had come from.

"What were you doing when it happened?"

"I had a headache and was trying to take a nap. When it

was time for the baby's bath, I asked Rob if he would do it just this once. Rob is wonderful with Gene, gets up at night, feeds him and plays with him and all the rest, but he hates to bathe or change him. I told him about the headache, though, and he agreed to do it. But when he came back it wasn't Rob. It was prot."

"How could you tell?"

"You already know the answer to that, Doctor B. Prot is different from Rob in a thousand ways."

"What did he say?"

"He said, 'Hiya, Giselle. So you're a mommy now.'"

"And you said—"

"I was too distressed to say much."

"So who gave the little guy his bath?"

"I think Rob probably started it, but never finished."

"And that's when prot appeared."

"I guess so. He never did get the diaper on right."

"I'm not surprised. He doesn't have much experience with babies, human or otherwise. What else can you tell me?"

"Nothing. Absolutely nothing. There he was, just as if he had never left."

"Did you ask him where Robert had gone?"

"Of course!" she wailed. Then, wistfully, "He didn't have a clue."

"He doesn't know where Robert is?"

That's when the tears came. I suppose Giselle hadn't thought about the full implication of this until that moment. It meant that Robert had retreated so deeply that not even his "guardian" (prot) knew where he was hiding. The baby started crying, too. She held him to her breast while I tried to reassure her. "We'll get to the bottom of it," I promised, without a lot of conviction. I thought we had already scraped out that barrel.

She nodded and found a handkerchief. I took little Gene, who smelled wonderfully piney, like his mother. He tweaked my nose. I feigned a roar of pain, which got him crying again, and only made things worse. "C'mon," I said to Giselle, after she had calmed herself and the boy. "Let's show Ward Two your new baby."

We found prot talking with the patients, some of whom obviously remembered him fondly. Frankie was there, fatter than ever and almost smiling, a rare occurrence for her. And Milton, whose entire family was wiped out in the holocaust, was quietly listening to whatever was being discussed, not joking or clowning around at all. Some of the others had never met prot, except by reputation, but were eagerly telling him their stories in a blatant, if pathetic, attempt to win a free trip to K-PAX, or at least to gain some sympathy for their plights. Half a dozen cats swarmed around him, too, purring and rubbing against his legs.

Of course most of the staff knew Giselle as well, and remembered her with equal affection. They were delighted to meet little Gene, and she seemed to break out of her funk for the moment. The baby, apparently unafraid of all the strange faces peering down at him, grinned up at everyone.

I took this opportunity to wade through the cats and ask prot whether he had any objection to checking back into the hospital "for a little R and R." Though he assured me he wasn't a bit tired, he nonetheless seemed overjoyed by the prospect. I suggested we meet at nine o'clock the next morning. He said he looked forward to another of our "fruitful" sessions together (the hint was not lost on me).

I bid him adieu and sought out Betty McAllister to request that she find a room for him, a private one where Giselle and the boy could comfortably visit. The most I could get from her was a nod indicating she understood my instruction; she was obviously more interested in the goings-on between the patients and the Porter family. By now Milton was standing on a table telling baby jokes, such as: "Woman gets on a bus with the ugliest baby in the world. Kid's so homely that all the other passengers are laughing at it. The woman starts to sob. Man gets on at the next stop, sees the woman crying and says to her, 'It can't be that bad. Have a peanut. And take one for your monkey.'"

With that I left them all and returned to my office to pull out prot/Robert's thick file once more and ponder all the frustrations and possibilities.

The next morning, while waiting for prot to arrive, I tried to imagine what might have occurred to trigger Robert's abrupt relapse to his sorry condition in 1990, i.e., an essentially catatonic state in which he hid from the world behind an alter ego who claimed to be from a distant planet.

It had happened, apparently, while he was bathing his four-and-a-half-month-old son. Could the baby's naked body have brought back all the suffering and terror imposed upon him by an abusive uncle when he, Robert, was a boy of five, something his own manifestly successful sex life had not precipitated? I cautioned myself not to jump to any such conclusion, though I hoped this was indeed the case. The alternative—that there was something in his early history even more devastating than these traumatic events, and the subsequent death of his beloved father—seemed far worse. Was there something we had not yet uncovered lurking in the depths of his psyche? Was the mind something like an onion, as some have suggested, revealing a new layer whenever one is peeled back, no matter how deeply we go?

The first thing prot did when he was escorted into my examining room was to remove his dark glasses (owing to the sensitivity of his eyes to visible light I kept the lamps dimmed when he was around) and go for the fruits I had provided for him. He was not disappointed. As a sort of "welcome home" gift I had filled the bowl with a cornucopia of all those available in the hospital kitchens, already cut up into bite-size pieces, as well as a napkin and fork, both of which he ignored. It was quite something, believe me, to watch him dig in, caution thrown to the winds, sucking everything up with noisy grunts and smacking sounds. When he was finished, and obviously satisfied, I suggested that it must have been a long time since he had tasted any fruit.

"Not really," he replied, licking the bristly beard surrounding his lips. "But I'll be leaving for home soon, and there won't be many more opportunities like this."

"You mean to K-PAX."

He nodded happily.

I remember feeling my throat tighten as I asked him when that might be.

Without the slightest hesitation he informed me that he would be departing Earth on December the thirty-first. At 11:48 in the morning, Eastern Standard Time, to be precise. "We won't be needing any lunch," he added wryly. Obviously cheerful and relaxed, he sat back in his chair, crossed his ankles, and placed his hands behind his head.

"Why the change of heart?"

"There's one of those peculiarly nonsensical expressions you humans are so fond of. A carryover from your muddled past, I assume." (He meant the history of our species, not my own.)

"Let me rephrase that. The last time you were here you refused to give me a date for your departure. Why is it no longer a secret?"

"My task here is almost finished. Everything is 'go,' and there is nothing you can do to screw things up, even if you wanted to."

This smug comment annoyed me. "What 'task'? Does it involve putting Robert back into a permanent catatonic state?"

"Really, gene, you humans shouldn't take things so seriously. Your lives are too short for that." On K-PAX, of course, there was no such problem: everyone lived to be a thousand.

I stared at him for a moment. "What have you done with Robert?"

"Not a thing. He's taking a break from his miserable life."

"Why? What happened?"

"No idea, coach."

"Then how do you know he's 'taking a break'?"

"He told me before he left."

"What else did he tell you?"

"That's about it."

"And you have no idea where he went?"

"Nope. He didn't say."

"If he shows up again, will you let me know?"

"*Mais oui, mon ami.*"

I was already beginning to get the feeling that I was not in control, that all I could do was make the best of things for the time being. "All right, let's talk about you for a minute."

"Fifty-nine, fifty-eight, fifty—"

"Very funny. Now—where have you been keeping yourself the past couple of years?"

"Oh, here and there."

"Prot, let me explain something. To you this whole thing might be a joke. The whole *world* may be a joke. But to Robert it's not funny. I would appreciate it if you would at least be more cooperative in answering my questions. Is that asking too much?"

He shrugged. "If you must know, I've been all around your WORLD (prot capitalized planets, stars, etc.; entities as trivial as people were, to him, lower case). Sort of a farewell tour, you might say."

"What was the purpose of this 'tour'? Were you entertaining the troops?"

"A few of them. But mainly I was speaking with various beings who want to go to K-PAX with me. I've only got room for a hundred of you. Oh—I told you that last time, didn't I?"

"You mean you've been—ah—selecting your 'travel companions'?"

"You could put it that way."

I casually reached for a ballpoint and some paper. "Do you mind telling me the names of some of the people on your list?"

Prot tilted the fruit bowl toward him, but it was as empty

13

as my yellow pad, except for a little juice, which he drank up. "A: Not all of them are people. And B: Yes, I do."

"Why?"

"You know the answer to that one, my human friend."

"You mean you're afraid we'll try to stop you from taking them with you, or talk them out of the trip—something like that."

"Well, *wouldn't* you?"

"Maybe," I admitted. "But mostly I wanted to contact one or two of them to see whether they could confirm your story. About being 'here and there' in the world, I mean."

"Would I lie to you, mr. district attorney? And anyway, you don't speak giraffe, do you? Or deer? I *know* you don't understand the languages of any of your sea beings—we've already determined that, remember?"

I could feel my frustration rising, along with my gorge, as it always did during our sessions together. "Well, how many of them are people?"

"Oh, a couple of dozen. Yours is the most unhappy species of all."

"Do any of them speak English?" I ventured.

"A few."

"But you won't let me talk to them."

"Feel free. But you'll have to figure out who they are for yourself."

"Any of them live here at the hospital?"

He grinned and said, "One or two, perhaps."

"I'll tell you what: You give me the name of just one of your passengers and I'll have the kitchen send up another bowl of fruit."

Apparently to signify that the subject was closed, he turned to study a watercolor of Vermont in the fall. "I remember that place," he murmured.

I jotted down a note to ask each of my patients whether they had been invited along for the ride to K-PAX, and to advise the rest of the staff to do the same. Not to help them get ready for the journey, but to prepare them for the disappointment of being left behind, jilted brides at an earthbound altar.

But there was still the matter at hand: where was Robert and why had he retreated so precipitously? Apparently we were to be given less than two months to get to the bottom of it all. I didn't much like the idea of being put under the gun again. "You say you're leaving us at the end of December—any way you can extend that?"

"Sorry."

"But you said last time you were here that there were three windows open for your return to K-PAX. Isn't this the second one?"

"Uh-uh. The second one already slipped by."

"So this is your last chance?"

"Yep."

"And if you didn't—"

"You got it. We'd be stuck here forever."

"How did you miss the second window?"

"Robert changed his mind again. He vacillates a lot."

I interrupted my doodling. "Robert is going with you this time?"

"If he still wants to. You know how it is. He's of three minds on the subject."

"So you've spoken to him since you disappeared two and a half years ago?"

"On occasion."

15

"Was that his idea or yours?"

"Mine, for the most part."

"Was it your idea to come back to New York this last time?"

"Nope. That was his."

"Why did he call you?"

"I guess he needed me."

"Why?"

"Didn't say." He stretched languorously, like a dog waking from a nap.

"Where were you when the call came, exactly? Can you tell me that?"

"Would you believe I was back in zaire? Of course it's called 'the democratic republic of congo' now." He shook his head. "People!"

"What were you doing in Congo?"

"Didn't we just discuss that? You've really got to do something with that memory of yours, gino!"

"Bear with me, prot. What was Robert doing when you showed up?"

"Giving his kid a bath."

"Did he finish it?"

"Nope. He handed me the washcloth and off he went."

"So you finished the bath?"

"I dried him off and stuck a diaper on him, if that's what you call those things. Then I put him back in his cage."

I stared at my pad, which produced only a date and time. "Prot, can you assure me that you'll stick around here until the thirty-first of December at—ah—11:48 A.M.?"

"Nope."

"Why the hell not?"

"Even at the speed of light it will take awhile to gather everyone up and get going."

"You mean you have to pick up all of your passengers one at a time? Like a bus driver? That's pretty primitive, isn't it?"

"The only alternative, herr doktor, would be to gather them up ahead of time. Which would create a number of other problems."

I crossed out 12/31. "All right, when will you be leaving exactly?"

"Probably right after breakfast."

I wrote down 12/31 again. "And you promise you won't leave the hospital until then?"

"Nope."

"Goddamn it, prot—why not?"

"I still have a few places to go."

"What places?"

"I've got to hand it to you, gene. You don't give up easily."

"Thank you—I'll take that as a compliment. So you won't share that information either?"

"Sorry."

"All right. Just sit back and relax. I'd like to speak to Robert now."

"Lotsa luck," he mumbled as his head dropped to his chest.

"Rob?" I waited. "Robert?"

Prot/Robert seemed to slouch down even further. There was no other detectable response.

"Robert, please come forward. I only want to speak to you for a second. Just to find out how you're feeling, what's bothering you so much. I helped you before, remember?"

17

Nothing.

"This room is your safe haven, just like it always was."

No response.

"You must be feeling pretty bad. But whatever it is, you can trust me. Will you just say 'Hello,' so I'll know you're here?"

Not a hint of movement.

"All right. Don't go anywhere. Just relax." I carefully opened the drawer of my desk and pulled out the whistle I had called him with under similar circumstances two years earlier. I blew it.

There was no response whatsoever.

"All right, Rob, we'll talk later. And if there's anything you want to discuss with me, just tell one of the nurses and I'll come running—okay? Now I'd like to speak with prot again. Prot? Are you here?"

At once his eyes opened and came to a focus on me. "Find him?"

"Not yet."

"That's the spirit," he said with his maddening grin, something between genuine warmth and cynical smirk.

"How long have you had that beard?" I asked him.

"A couple of your years. I may keep it. What do you think?"

"Did you know that Rob has a beard exactly like yours?"

"Will wonders never cease!"

"You don't see any connection between his and yours?"

"Why should I?"

I stared at him glumly. "Prot, I'm going to ask you a favor."

"Very human of you, doc."

"I'm going to ask you to help me get through to Robert. Like you did a couple of years ago, remember?"

"That was different. He *wanted* to come out then. I couldn't have stopped him even if I'd tried."

"All I'm asking is that you talk to him, do whatever you can to help him *want* to get whatever's bothering him off his chest. Will you do that?"

"Sure, boss. If I see him. But I can't guarantee anything."

"Just do your best. That's all I ask."

He shrugged. "Don't I always?"

We sat staring at each other. Finally I asked whether he had had a chance to talk to any of the other patients about their problems.

"Some of them."

"Any thoughts so far?"

"Yes."

"Want to give me a summary?"

"No."

Annoyed, I tossed my pad onto the desk. "All right. That's all for today." I consulted my calendar, but for purposes of form only. I had already decided to give prot/Robert as much time as I could manage. I only wished there were more. "We'll meet every Tuesday and Friday at nine. All right with you?"

"What's the matter with Monday, Wednesday and Thursday?"

"Prot, you're not the only resident of MPI, unfortunately."

"I'll bet you say that to all your patients."

"Not really. Okay then, I'll see you again on Tuesday. In the meantime, I'll set up an appointment for your entrance, or re-entrance, physical with Dr. Chakraborty. Okay?"

"Why? My health is good. Don't feel a day over two hundred and fifty."

"Just routine," I assured him.

"Ah, yes. I remember your penchant for routine."

"Fine. Then I'll see you next week." I got up to escort him to the door.

"*Auf wiedersehen!*" he cried as he hurried out, apparently eager to get back to Ward Two. The room he was going to, incidentally, had been vacated not long before by another patient with a tragic history. Six months earlier the man, who was affectionately dubbed "Mr. Magoo," had suddenly stopped recognizing faces, including his own. Unfortunately, the problem had a physical etiology (he had been beaned by a falling brick), and there wasn't much we could do for him except to encourage his family, friends, and co-workers to wear name tags at all times. His wife, however, rebelled against this idea and, perhaps understandably, was gone by the time he returned to their apartment.

I plopped back down in my chair and looked over my meager notes for this session. "12/31, right after breakfast," and "Check with patients about their plans re: K-PAX," I read, along with a half-page of undecipherable doodles, tangled blue strings in a dull-yellow matrix. I only hoped the threads winding through Robert's mind could be unraveled and put into some kind of order before it was too late. The last time prot "departed" under similar circumstances Rob was left in a catatonic state from which he didn't emerge for five years, when his alter ego paid a return visit. But this time he wouldn't be coming back.

The only good news arising from our encounter was Robert's telling prot he was only "taking a break from his miserable life," suggesting that, when the time was right, he might again be ready to cooperate in a treatment program. But when would that be? And why was he suddenly so miserable? I only hoped we could do more for him than for the patient who had just vacated his room, though we had precious little time to do it in.

I returned to my inner office, where Giselle was waiting. I had almost forgotten she was there.

"Well?" she demanded, though it was more like a bleat.

"I'm sorry, Giselle, it looks as though we're back to square one."

"But why? I don't understand."

"Sometimes a mental illness comes like a bolt of lightning. Literally. Some little spark seems to set off a whole cascade of electrical events. Until we know a lot more about the chemistry and physics of the brain, all we can do is try to get the patient back on track by whatever means is available."

She frowned. Having traveled down this road before, she knew the risks and probabilities as well as I. "Can I have access to him like you've given me in the past?"

"Of course." I had no intention of arguing with that request, as I had before. In view of her unique position as a sort of buffer between prot (Robert) and the outside world, we both knew she could be extremely helpful to all of us. Perhaps he would utter something significant when she was around, something that none of the nurses would recognize as important. "By the way, where's your son?"

"I called my mom last night. She's staying with us until we figure out what's going on."

"What about Rob's mother?"

"I called her, too. She's remarried, and living in Arizona now. She wanted to come, but I talked her out of it. There wouldn't be much point in her visiting him if we don't know where he is."

I gazed at her eager, still-youthful face. "You probably know as much about Rob's problem as I do, Giselle. What do *you* think went wrong?"

"I suppose giving Gene his bath somehow brought everything back. But why he left so abruptly and prot came back at exactly the same time . . ." She shrugged.

I had forgotten that she considered them to be two separate individuals. "Any idea where he might have gone?"

"None at all. Unless he went back to Guelph."

"His home town?"

"Yes."

"Why Guelph?"

"I don't know. When I'm overwhelmed with something, it helps to go back to the place I grew up in. It's like returning to a simpler time, I suppose."

I nodded understandingly though I, myself, still lived in the house I grew up in, and had nowhere else to go. But neither my own childhood nor Giselle's were fraught with the misery that had befallen Robert's.

"Can I go see him now?"

"All right, Giselle. Go see what you can find out from prot that I can't."

"Thanks, Doctor B." She jumped up and pecked me on the cheek before skipping out. In another second she skipped back in. "By the way," she added. "Would you be willing to take care of Oxie until Rob comes back?"

As it happened, our own Dalmatian, Shasta Daisy, had died in August. Though she was nearly fifteen and had had a wonderfully happy life, we still missed her sleeping with us, watching everything from the back seat of the car, playing with the grandkids. Giselle had me again and she knew it.

"All right. Bring him in tomorrow and I'll take him home with me."

"Just one thing."

"What's that?"

"He's a vegetarian now."

"The dog? Is that possible?"

"Sure. It's just a matter of feeding him the right nutrients in the right proportions. I'll give you a list."

"Thanks," I mumbled.

She smiled brightly. "I knew I could count on you."

I only wished I could share her confidence.

After Giselle had gone I found myself trying vainly to reorganize the piles of paper strewn all over my desk, a ritual I go through every time some unexpected and unwanted new burden is tossed onto it. There were unrefereed manuscripts, unattended meeting invitations, an unfinished paper of my own, books, reprints, catalogs, notebooks, yellow pads, Post-its and memos of all kinds. At the back of it all stood a picture of my entire family.

I gazed lovingly at the photo, remembering the event at which it was taken, a backyard picnic more than seven years ago, the time I first invited prot to the house to determine the effect of a normal home environment on his condition (I didn't know about Rob at the time). My wife Karen and I are seated in the foreground, Shasta at our feet, backed by our sons Fred on the left and Will on the right, with daughters Abby and Jennifer standing between them. It's Will's fingers that form the antenna sticking up from the back of my head.

How much things change in seven years! Will, who was in high school at the time and suffering through a nearly catastrophic cocaine addiction, is now in his third year of medical school and doing exceedingly well. He is still planning a career in psychiatry, and he and his fiancée Dawn Siegel plan to be married as soon as he graduates (they've already been living together for two years).

Jennifer, a medical student herself at the time the picture was taken, is now specializing in the treatment and prevention of HIV infections in the San Francisco area. In fact, she has become something of a celebrity in Northern California, the subject of several newspaper and magazine articles, and is as happy in her dismal work as was Mother Teresa in hers. Though her responsibilities preclude her visiting us more than once or twice a year, we are, of course, extremely proud of her great success and dedication.

That was a year of transition for Fred, who continues to amaze us with his career as a singer and actor. He has appeared in a couple of films and soap operas, but spends most of his time on stage, and, in fact, made his first Broadway appearance last year in the smash hit *Rent* and is now in the road company of *Les Misérables* (we didn't even know he could sing until we saw him perform at a dinner theater in Newark not long after the picture was taken). Freddy lives in the East Village with a beautiful ballerina, but refuses to discuss the possibility of marriage, at least not with us. His mother continues to hope, however.

I turned my gaze on Abby, the eldest of the four, and the most outspoken. Now approaching forty, she remains active in a number of causes, particularly that of animal rights, which she claims is the coming thing. "People are beginning to realize that animals have their own feelings and sensitivities, sometimes not very different from our own," she insists. She is prot's favorite, I suspect.

Our astronomer son-in-law Steve (who took the picture) and his colleague Charles Flynn were, of course, instrumental in uncovering prot's vast knowledge of astronomical matters, including his identifying several planets associated with solar systems elsewhere in the galaxy. Indeed, Dr. Flynn has long been convinced that prot is, in fact, from the planet K-PAX.

But back to the family: Steve and Abby's children Rain and Star, now thirteen and eleven and glued to their computer monitors several hours a day, have turned into surprisingly normal adolescents, bright yet thoughtful and considerate. Rain, in fact, is planning on becoming an Eagle Scout, and has already earned several merit badges along the way. Though we see Abby's family more often than the others, we still don't see them often enough. We don't see any of them often enough.

Perhaps that will change with the new year. Karen, thanks primarily to the option payments on the film version of K-PAX, decided to retire at the end of the year. She already has our travel plans worked out for the next three decades and persistently reminds me that the longer I work the less time we will have left. "What about my patients?" I ask her.

"You can't stay at the hospital forever," she always tells me. "You've got to leave them to someone else sooner or later."

It's not that easy, of course, though I see her point. Sometimes I almost think it would be nice to have a multiple personality, to be able to lead two lives (or more) at the same time. Most of us, however, are stuck with just the one. I could only hope mine could be of some benefit to Robert Porter, to help him get to the bottom of his difficulty and start him again on the long road to a permanent recovery.

SESSION THIRTY-FOUR

I BROUGHT Oxeye home with me on Saturday. Karen was delighted to see him and, for that matter, so was everyone else (the Dalmatian, which I had given to Rob in a fruitless attempt to lure him out of his catatonic state, had lived with us from 1991–5). In fact, Abby and her family came up from Princeton for the occasion.

My daughter seemed to have mellowed in the last couple of years, hardly bugging me at all about her hopelessly liberal causes. Maybe she was just glad to be back home for a while. Or perhaps it had something to do with her fortieth birthday looming on the horizon. Oxie, for his part, was also happy to be with us, though he sniffed hard for Shasta and whined for a time when he couldn't find her (we buried her in her favorite spot at our summer place in the Adirondacks).

Rain and Star ran all over the yard with him that afternoon while the old folks chatted inside. Despite the negative aspects of prot's return, everyone was overjoyed that he was back as well, and hoped I would bring him home for a cookout, the setting for their earlier encounters with him.

"In the winter?" I protested.

Karen pointed out that Thanksgiving and Christmas were coming up. "Maybe you could bring him home for those."

I didn't even want to think about that. It seemed as though we had only put away the decorations a short time before.

I cornered my son-in-law Steve and asked him about his colleague, Charlie Flynn, who had recently returned from Libya (by special dispensation from Colonel Qaddafi in return for a percentage of any profits) with a tiny supply of spider excrement indigenous to that country. According to prot, this was a key component in a cold fusion reaction. Though the results of a single small experiment (in collaboration with the physics department) looked promising, the amount, unfortunately, was insufficient to catalyze a larger-scale production. Undeterred, Flynn was busy gathering feces from various native American arachnid species in hopes of isolating the key element in this material, which could well solve the world's energy problems, not to mention his own financial ones.

"Ah think he's in Mexico now, trackin' down tarantulas," Steve chuckled.

I asked him whether there had been any developments in the study of planet K-PAX and its double star system.

"Well, another of our faculty has found what looks to be a second planet in that solar system. Ah wonder why prot never mentioned it to you."

"Maybe he doesn't know about it."

"Ah wouldn't be too sure. Anyway, you might ask him. It's even bigger than K-PAX. The main difference is that it orbits far outside the double star system, not inside it like K-PAX does."

"I'll do that."

At that point Rain showed up. Now a teenager, his voice had already changed and he sported a feeble mustache, which he's decided to keep. He seemed to have shot up another several inches since we had last seen him, and was almost as tall as I was. I felt a little like "Albert Einstein," one of my patients at MPI, who was desperately trying to slow down time and could only watch helplessly as it rolled on and on, carrying him, and the rest of us, along with it like some invisible avalanche. Of course this only reminded me that the time for prot's departure was lurking, like a giant boulder, at the bottom of the mountain.

After the death of our former director, Klaus Villers, I was voted acting director of the hospital in the fall of 1997. Following interviews with a number of candidates for the permanent directorship, some of whom were crazier than the patients, it was clear that the best person for the job was our own Virginia Goldfarb. Though she has a few figurative warts, as do we all, she is even-handed and fair, and makes decisions only after careful deliberation and weighing of all the options. Moreover, she keeps herself informed of developments in many areas of psychiatry, including her own specialties, bipolar disorder and megalomania. Finally, she practically squeaks of confidence and self-assurance, which doesn't hurt in the fund-raising department, and I think she was a fine choice to lead the Manhattan Psychiatric Institute into the twenty-first century (though I wasn't too pleased that she put me in charge of the committee supervising the construction of the new wing, which takes a whopping amount of time).

At the regular Monday morning staff meeting, chaired by Dr. Goldfarb, there was a great deal of interest in prot's return and what it might tell us not only about Robert Porter's condition, but about others suffering from the bizarre affliction known as multiple personality disorder (MPD) as well. Although regression to the various individual personalities is not an uncommon occurrence, the patient can usually be reintegrated more easily the second time around. In the case of Robert/prot, however, the problem was complicated by the disappearance of the principal alter.

That led to a discussion of what it means to be an alter ego, i.e., how does a secondary or other personalities differ from the primary one, and from the fully integrated human being? Are they completely different individuals? Or are certain things missing in the thoughts and feelings of the various alters, who are merely "parts" of a whole? Are we all simply a mix of different personalities which dominate our minds at different times? If so, which of these is responsible for our actions? All very interesting, I remarked, but what specific recommendations were there in the case of my relapsed patient, Robert Porter?

Ron Menninger pointed out that MPD differs from all the other syndromes in that aggressive drug treatment of the individual at hand, while perhaps beneficial to him, can be devastating to one or more of the other egos (at this point I wasn't even certain how many others there were in Robert's case), and perhaps to the integrated personality as a whole.

A consensus was reached that I should continue psycho-analysis, at least for a while, in hopes that probing into prot's psyche might provide further information about what had happened to Robert, his primary alter, much as it had seven years earlier. For example, prot's abhorrence of money in particular, and capitalism in general, seemed to be related to the severe financial obligations incurred by Rob's family following the fatal injury of his father.

While all this was debatable, unanimous agreement was reached on one thing: no TV appearances for prot this time! Letters and calls from people who wanted to meet him or make use of his talents or follow him to a distant planet were still dribbling in more than two years after he was interviewed on a television talk show. More disturbingly, there were several communications from people in various countries who claimed they had seen him, and even a few who insisted that he had taken them aboard his space ship and examined them. A woman in France claimed she was pregnant with his child! Obviously she hadn't heard about prot's tremendous aversion to the procreation process, which was intimately related, of course, to Robert's sexual abuse as a child.

This was followed by a preliminary discussion of a possible replacement for Carl Thorstein, who was interviewing for a position elsewhere. And we had only just found someone (Laura Chang) to take the place of Klaus Villers, who had died at about the time of prot's "disappearance" in 1995.

The subject turned, finally, to a couple of the other problem patients. One of these, the aforementioned "Albert Einstein," is a Chinese–American physicist who believes that time not only flies, but is accelerating! Quite successful in his career until several months ago, he broke down while presenting a paper on the nature of time at an international scientific meeting.

We all harbor the illusion that time moves faster as we grow older. At that conference Albert hypothesized that this is indeed a physical fact having something to do with the expansion of the universe. He tearfully reported to the shocked scientists that time was literally speeding up, that life was rapidly passing him by, along with his audience and all the rest of us. After seeing his own psychiatrist he was taken to "the Big Institute" at Columbia, where he was treated vigorously, though without success, with electroshock and other therapies, and finally ended up with us. He now spends most of his time in his room, along with dozens of pencils and reams of paper, in feverish pursuit of the impossible—of finding a way to slow down time mathematically, or even stop it altogether. Ironically, when he becomes too tired to think, he sits quietly and does nothing at all, in an attempt to make the minutes crawl by as slowly as possible. Like many of our residents, he sleeps very little. Obviously in great anguish, he moans and fidgets during every analytic session and finally jumps up and runs to the door, hoping somehow to make up for lost time.

Another patient under review was a woman suffering from an unusual form of schizophrenia, or perhaps a previously unreported type of bipolar disorder (formerly called manic depression). The patient, a woman we call Alice, sometimes sees herself as no bigger than an insect in a world of giants. At such times she is terrified of being stepped on, drowning in a cup of tea, being eaten by one of the cats, and so on. At others she thinks she has become gigantic, all-powerful, utterly in control of everything around her, including the staff and the other patients. At still other times she seems perfectly normal in every way, continually pestering her doctor (Goldfarb) to "let me out of this madhouse." We don't have a clue as to the cause of this curious affliction, nor that of various other phobias, compulsions, and social deviations, whose victims haven't been helped in the slightest by even the newest and most powerful neuroleptic drugs.

Carl Beamish joined Goldfarb in suggesting that prot might have a talk with some of these problem patients. In fact, I suspect this was the reason for their being included on the meeting's agenda. There were no objections, except by me. I protested, as I had earlier, that although he had shown an amazing ability to help such unfortunates in the past, our primary responsibility was to Robert and *his* treatment. Indeed, we seemed to be back where we had started in 1990, with no clear idea of what underlay Robert's difficulty in dealing with the world around him, or how to get to the bottom of it. However, I did agree to question prot about his prognoses for the other patients, while, at the same time, requesting that everyone present query their charges about their future travel plans.

My main concern, however, was in reintegrating prot's powerful personality into that of Robert Porter's so that his family could once again be reunited, Giselle could have her husband back, and baby Gene his missing father.

Prot seemed cheerful and relaxed when he came into my examining room the following morning. "Happy Veterans Day!" he cried as he went for a pear. I watched him eat the whole thing, seeds and all, smacking his lips as usual in what was at once a delightful and disgusting spectacle.

"You know about Veterans Day?"

"Only that it used to be called Armistice Day. But you changed it because it sent the wrong message."

"What message?"

Munch, munch, munch. "That peace is a good thing. You prefer to honor your warriors. Makes it easier to recruit the next batch, don'tcha know." A speck of the Bartlett flew across the room.

"You think we're a violent, warlike species, don't you?"

He stared at me in some amusement. "Well, if you ain't, why do you teach your children the 'glories' of destroying your 'enemies'?"

"I didn't teach my children—"

"You sent them to school, didn't you? They watched TV, didn't they? You even took them to Gettysburg! What were they to think about all those heroic battles in all those wars?"

I gazed at him sitting in the dim light, one of his legs drawn up under him disarmingly. "Tell me—did Robert have a set of toy soldiers?"

"I saw some of them on my first visit."

"That's the only time?"

"Yep."

"Later on—did he have any problem with the military?"

His eyebrows came up. "How on EARTH should I know?"

"He never mentioned anything about wanting to go into the military or, maybe, ways to keep out of it?"

"Nope. Never did."

I made a note to find out whether a friend or relative of Rob's had died in Vietnam. Or perhaps the killer of his wife and daughter had been wearing part of a military uniform when Robert encountered him.

As prot sank his teeth into another pear I asked him how he felt about being back at MPI. "You've added some new patients since I was here—interesting beings in every ward!"

I reminded myself to follow up on this appraisal as soon as time permitted. "Dr. Chakraborty tells me you're still in excellent shape for a man your age."

He smiled. "I told you that—remember?"

I didn't argue the matter. Mainly I had wanted to get a blood sample to compare with an earlier one, which suggested, unless someone had gotten the tubes mixed up (this happens more often than you might imagine), that his DNA was quite different from Robert's. In any case, we would have the results in a few weeks.

"You remember Steve, my son-in-law?" I asked him.

"Sure Ah do. The astronomer."

"He tells me there's another planet orbiting K-MON and K-RIL. Is that right?"

"No. That's *not* right."

"It's not??"

"That's what I said. In fact, there are *eight* others. Most are too small to detect from EARTH with the primitive methods you insist on using."

"Why didn't you tell me about these planets before?"

"My dear sir, you never *asked*."

"Well, are any of them inhabited?"

"I assume you mean by people?"

"By life of any kind."

"Nope. Except for the occasional visitor, of course."

"In other words, your solar system is very similar to ours."

"Naturally."

"Don't you find that interesting?"

He ignored the implication of this astute observation. "Not particularly. For your information, doc, and that of your astronomer relatives, most solar systems around the GALAXY conform to this pattern. But only about one PLANET in five hundred supports the kind of life you're talking about."

I smiled at him, perhaps a bit too knowingly. "Just for the record, though, do all of those solar systems have nine planets?"

He ignored the condescending grin, too. "No, and neither does yours. Many STARS have no PLANETARY COMPANIONS at all. Others have a hundred or more. The average is about a dozen. Not counting all the little rocks you call 'asteroids,' of course."

"Did you say the Earth doesn't have nine planets?"

"There are a few out beyond PLUTO you haven't found yet."

There was no way to argue this point, so I let it drop. "Hear anything from Rob?"

"Not a peep."

"And you still have no idea where he might be?"

"Nary a clue."

"Could you find him if you wanted to?"

"Maybe. But he obviously doesn't want to be found, does he?"

"Prot, I'm going to ask you another favor."

"Here we go again."

"I'm going to ask you to look hard for him. And when you find him, to give him this message: Tell him I won't bother him right now; Giselle and I just want to get some information from him. Whether he wants to stay in graduate school, for example. After that he can go back to wherever he's been keeping himself. Will you do that?"

"Pretty devious trick if you ask me, doc." He crunched up and swallowed the last of a core. "All right. I'll see what I can do."

"Thank you, prot. I appreciate that."

"No problemo." With a straight face he added, "Where do you suggest I look?"

I studied him, not knowing whether he was joking or not. Sometime during the middle of a sleepless night, I had gotten a feeble idea. I told him I would like to speak to Paul now.

"Should I think pleasant thoughts or something?"

"Sure, if you like. Think about sailing over K-PAX in a balloon or pitching to Babe Ruth or something." He closed his eyes and smiled happily, for all the world as if he were in the middle of some high adventure.

I waited for a moment. "Paul? Will you come forward please?" (Paul was the alter ego who first appeared when Robert reached puberty and, because of his earlier abuses, was unable to handle the sexual impulses of normal adolescence, for which prot was of no help whatsoever. He went on to volunteer his services with Rob's late wife, Sarah.)

Prot shifted slightly in his chair, but Paul made no appearance.

"You might as well come on out, Paul," I told him. "I can bring you forward with hypnosis any time I want."

I wasn't certain of that, but Paul was convinced, apparently. His eyes slowly opened and he stretched lazily. "Oh, hello, doc. How are things?"

I gazed into his eyes. Like prot's they were playful, mischievous. "You remember the last time we chatted? It was a couple of years ago."

"Like it was yesterday."

"What have you been up to since that time?"

"Not much."

"You haven't made an appearance since Rob left the hospital?"

"Only a couple of times a week."

I was somewhat taken aback by this matter-of-fact reply. "Really? What do you do when you come out?"

"Oh, this and that. Try to satisfy Giselle's needs, for the most part. Don't let that innocent look fool you—she's a tiger in bed. Or tigress . . . ?"

I was crestfallen. If Paul was, in fact, assuming Rob's conjugal duties at this late date, he had probably been doing so in 1995. In that case, was Robert in on the deception? Why would he want to pretend that he was making such terrific progress when he was, in fact, still as miserable as ever? Had he been using his apparent "recovery" to distract us from something even worse than his profound sexual dysfunction?

There was nothing to do but take things as they came. "Are you aware of everything Rob has been up to during the last two years?"

"More or less. He studies a lot. Dull stuff. I usually sleep when he does that. Love to sleep."

"Bully for you," I said enviously. "But you're aware of what's going on with him most of the time—is that right?"

"Okay. Okay. I have eavesdropped on Rob's private life. I need to be ready if he fails to live up to his obligations. You understand."

"Yes, I think I do, finally." In fact, I felt like a damn fool, and almost said so. "Anything else to report? Anything you've seen or heard that his doctor ought to know about?"

He scratched his chin and contemplated the ceiling. "Can't think of a thing, doc. All of his equipment seems to work okay."

"What about last Thursday? Were you aware that Rob called on prot to return?"

"Sure—I couldn't miss something as obvious as that."

"What was he doing at the time?"

"Giving the kid—my kid—a bath. He's a slippery little bastard."

"Anything happen while he was doing that? Did Rob suddenly become ill, or did he cry out, or faint—anything like that?"

"Not a thing. All at once prot was there and Rob wasn't."

"Who finished the bath?"

"Prot, I s'pose. What's the difference?"

"I don't know. Do you have any thoughts on that?"

He pondered this. "Not really."

"Well, do you know where Rob went?"

"Nope. When this happens he can stay away for ages, damn him."

"Why 'damn him'?"

"Are you kidding? No Rob, no pussy wussy."

"Paul, when did Rob first call you?"

"He was—I don't know—twelve or thirteen, I guess. Something like that."

"And you've been around ever since?"

"From time to time."

"Exactly how often did he call you, and under what circumstances?"

"I told you—he needed someone to take over whenever he got an erection and had to do something about it."

"With girls?"

"With himself, mostly."

"And later on, with girls."

"Nope. Only one girl. What was her name again? Oh, yeah. Sarah. Only he called her Sally. A little dippy, but a good lay." His smile was not like prot's—there was an element of sarcasm in it. "Different from Giselle. I imagine all women are different. I've only had two." He sat up straighter, looked directly at me (until then his eyes had shifted from place to place, never focusing on anything for more than a few seconds) and winked. "You'd probably know more about that than I would. . . ."

He was quite wrong about that, but I wasn't about to go into it. "So you just—what—lie around and wait for the right moment?"

"That's about it."

"What about Harry? What has he been up to?"

"That little shit? Haven't heard from him in a long time."

"And as I recall, there's no one else there with you besides Rob, prot, and Harry—is that right?"

"I already told you that a couple of years ago. You hounded Rob like this, too, and look what happened."

"All right, Paul, that's all for today. You can go back to sleep now."

He yawned. "So long, doc. By the way, you got any other patients that need some help? I'm horny as hell."

"I'll let you know."

He shrugged, nodded, and his eyes slowly closed.

I was not unhappy to see this somewhat disgusting young man, who seemed to be interested in little besides sex, withdraw. Perhaps this said more about my own hangups than his promiscuity, but I had no time to dwell on the matter. Before prot could make a reappearance, I asked Harry to come forward. (It was Harry who took over whenever Rob was being abused by his uncle. Indeed, there is reason to believe that it was he, not Robert, who killed the murderer of his wife and daughter, perhaps confusing him for Uncle Dave.) It took a while, but he finally opened his eyes and looked around the room, blinking, presumably trying to figure out where he was.

"Hi, Harry. How are you doing?" The picture of a five-year-old boy with a beard had a somewhat comical effect.

"Okay, I guess." He frowned. "You're that doctor, aren't you?"

"You remember me?"

"What happened to your beard?" Oblivious to his own, he rubbed his nose and wiped his finger on his pants.

"Oh, I've got it in a jar at home."

His eyes widened, but he said nothing.

"What have you been up to the last couple of years?"

"Just waitin', keepin' an eye out."

"For Uncle Dave?"

41

"Yeah."

"Do you mind if I ask you some questions?"

He shuffled his feet. "I guess not."

"Were you around when prot came back this time?"

He felt the vinyl arms of his chair. "Who's 'prot'?"

"Never mind. Were you there when Rob left last week?"

"Uh-huh."

"What happened?"

Another frown. "I dunno." His nose seemed plugged, as if he had a cold. "He was givin' somebody a bath."

"And he left without any warning?"

"I guess so."

"Any idea where he went?"

He looked around the room. "No," he said, though it sounded more like "dough."

"All right. Did I ask you before whether you know about anyone else who lives with you and Rob?"

He shrugged. "I don't remember."

"Well, *do* you?"

"No."

"What about Paul?"

"Huh?"

"You've never met Paul?"

He fidgeted with his shirt buttons. "Uh-uh."

"Or anyone else besides Robin?" (Robert's childhood name.)

"Uh-uh."

"Anything else you want to tell me about Rob while you're here?"

He wagged his head.

"All right, Harry. You can go."

He looked around one last time before closing his eyes.

Again I waited for prot to reappear, but he just sat there, apparently asleep.

"Prot?"

His eyes popped open. "Present and accounted for."

"Did you hear any of my conversations with Paul and Harry?"

"Not a word. Did I miss anything?"

"Apparently you've missed quite a lot. Both of us have. All right. Our time's about up. You might as well go back to Ward Two."

"So early?" He grabbed the last pear on his way to the door. "See you Friday," he called out.

"Wait a second. I almost forgot." I retrieved a weighty bundle, held together by two enormous rubber bands, that the mail room had sent over. "This is all the stuff that came for you while you were gone. We didn't know where to forward it," I added pointedly.

Ignoring the comment he took the package. "Thanks, doc." He riffled through some of the letters. "I hope none of these beings want to go to K-PAX. The passenger list is just about filled up."

As he left, I marveled at the confidence he exuded, his conviction that he was, in fact, a K-PAXian. There wasn't a shred of doubt in his mind. But neither is there any (in the patients' minds) that our current "Christ" is the son of God, that our resident "Croesus" is a rich and powerful woman, or that any of our other delusionals are not who they think they are. For that matter, all of us probably harbor a number of delusions, thinking ourselves more or less attractive, smarter or dumber than we really are. On the other hand, perhaps we are all exactly who we think we are. Prot is right about one thing: truth is whatever we believe it to be.

The idea I had come up with the previous night wasn't just feeble, it was decrepit. Except for the revelation that Rob had been faking his all-too-rapid recovery in 1995, neither Paul nor Harry were going to be of much help in finding out what happened the week before. Paul appeared to be little interested in Rob, much less prot, unless there was some sexual gratification in it; and Harry, who was only five, was apparently unaware of the existence of the other personalities, except, of course, for Robert. Unless there were someone in there I didn't yet know about, all I had left was prot.

But even he didn't seem particularly eager to work with Rob this time around, perhaps because of the latter's (from prot's point of view) intransigence. He had already spent several years trying to convince Robert to leave the world he was unable to deal with and return with him to the idyllic planet K-PAX, to no avail.

The questions still remained: What had happened to Robert, and why *then*? What did it have to do with bathing the baby, if anything? On top of that dilemma, how was I going to tell Giselle that she had been sleeping with two different men, and that Paul, not Rob, was the father of little Gene? The old retirement bug began buzzing around my ears, and I didn't try very hard to swat it away. I almost felt sorry for Will, now well into his third year of medical school. But I remembered my own student days, and those difficult, exciting years of residency. If I had the chance all over again, I'd probably do exactly the same thing, make the same damn mistakes, take the bad with the good.

*　　*　　*

After letting prot go a few minutes early I seized the opportunity to take a stroll on the grounds. For one thing I wanted to get a look at progress on the construction of the new wing, the Klaus M. and Emma R. Villers Laboratory for Experimental Therapy and Rehabilitation. More importantly, I have come to realize over the years that a great deal can be learned from informal encounters with the patients. The more contact we have with them the better we are able to spot subtle changes in their behavior, something that might be missed in the more formal setting of the examining room. Besides, it was a sunny November day, and there weren't going to be many as pleasant for some time.

On this particular occasion I found Ophelia sitting with Alex on a bench not far from the side entrance, and I ambled over to speak with them. Ophelia is a young woman who will do anything anyone tells her to. An orphan who was passed from one foster home to another, she became obsessed early in life with trying to please her various parents so they wouldn't dump her off on someone else. Like an anorectic, who can never be thin enough, she blamed herself for each perceived failure, and tried harder and harder to please everyone. Ironically, this blatantly sycophantic behavior drove away many prospective parents. At the same time, she suffered abuse from teachers and students, employers and co-workers in whatever situation she found herself. Eventually she learned to trust no one, while helplessly complying with every wish or command. She ended up with us when she was found wandering in Central Park after having been raped by a shoe salesman.

With her was another patient whom we call "Alex Trebek,"

after the host of the popular television quiz show, *Jeopardy*. Perhaps because the real Mr. Trebek makes his job look so easy, our "Alex" firmly believes that he (or perhaps anyone) can do it as well as the original, and, indeed, has offered to substitute for Mr. Trebek, without notice, at any time. As with the route to Carnegie Hall, he thinks he can get there with practice, and he roams the wards and grounds shouting "Yes!" and "That's right!" and "Correct!" This in itself would not place him with us. The problem with "Alex" is that these are the only words he utters.

As with most mental patients, there is a lighter side to all this. With his mustache and sporty jacket and tie he even looks a little like the real game-show host, and many of our visitors become convinced that Alex Trebek himself is a resident of MPI, no matter what denials we might make.

I paused at their bench and asked if either had spoken with prot as yet. Ophelia inquired immediately (so I wouldn't think she was being recalcitrant, I suppose) whether I thought that would be a good idea. "Doesn't make any difference to me," I assured her. "I was just curious."

She admitted she had talked with prot for a few minutes over the weekend.

"Correct!" confirmed Alex.

"And did he ask you whether you wanted to go to K-PAX?"

"Would you be unhappy if I told you he did?"

"No."

"We all want to go," she confessed matter-of-factly. "But he can only take a hundred of us with him."

"You are right!"

At this point one of our "exhibitionists" darted from behind

46

a tree and exposed a bare foot to us. When no one responded, he grabbed his shoe and slunk off.

"Well, did he give you any encouragement?"

"Would that be wrong?"

"No."

"He said the trip is still open to anyone. The passenger list hasn't been finalized yet."

"Do you want to be on it?"

"Would it annoy you if I said 'yes'?"

"Either answer would be fine."

"I told him that I would be happy to do whatever he wanted me to do."

"That's it!" Alex shouted.

Seeing Cassandra leave her favorite spot not far away, I excused myself and hurried to catch up. As always, Ophelia seemed distressed that I was leaving her, feeling, I suppose, that she had displeased me in some way.

But I needed to speak with our resident prophet, whose ability to predict future events could be of help in determining what prot had in mind for the other patients. "Hello, Cassandra!" I called out.

She stopped and tried to focus on the reality of my appearance.

I couldn't help but notice that she seemed a little down. "Anything wrong, Cassie?"

She stared at me for a few minutes before turning and wandering slowly away. I didn't like the look of that. It usually meant she had seen signs in the sky suggesting that something bad was going to happen. If so, there was no way I could get her to tell me what it was until she was ready to do so.

At this point Milton appeared. "Man comes home to find his house burned to the ground. 'Damn!' he says. 'I miss everything!'"

When I didn't laugh, he brought out three huge seeds, taken from one of the dried-out sunflowers lining the back wall, and began to juggle them. I watched Cassandra dissolve in a group of other patients, all huddled around the fountain (which had been turned off for the winter months) like a flock of sheep. Among those present were "Joan of Arc," who doesn't understand the meaning of the word "fear," and "Don Knotts," who is afraid of everything. It suddenly occurred to me that their illnesses might be related to MPD, that their "incomplete" psyches might be akin to part of a multiple personality, the other alter(s) being absent or repressed. I stood there wishing we could somehow integrate these two patients, and some of the others milling around the "back forty," to create new, and perhaps whole, individuals out of those whose psyches had become dominated by one emotion or another. But that, along with our understanding of how prot managed to "disappear" on certain occasions, would have to wait until some future time.

Milton was still juggling sunflower seeds when I left, sometimes off his foot and around his back. He was amazingly good, actually.

Giselle was waiting for me when I returned to my office (we had agreed to meet after each Tuesday session to compare notes). I told her about K-PAX's supposed companion planets, and about the letters I had passed on to prot.

She wasn't much interested in these revelations. "He told me yesterday that he hasn't found Rob yet. Did he have any luck today?"

"Unfortunately, no. But he promised me he would make a serious effort to do so."

She seemed disappointed with our lack of progress, as, of course, was I.

"Giselle, you knew this wasn't going to be easy. In my opinion something is bothering Robert that may be even more devastating to him than the sexual abuse by his uncle and the murder of his wife and daughter, if you can believe there could be anything worse than that. It may have something to do with bathing your son."

She thought about this. "My God—you mean he was abused when he was a *baby*?"

"No, no, no, I didn't say that. But if something did happen at that early age, it's not going to be easy to get to. Even if Robert were here and willing to cooperate it would be almost impossible."

"You mean we may *never* know what happened to him?"

"I didn't say that, either. I said it's going to be very difficult. Besides, it may have nothing to do with his bathing your son."

"So what can we do?"

"All we can do is keep prot talking, encourage him to get through to Robert, and go from there. But," I cautioned her, "don't press him too hard on this. Just talk with him about whatever he wants to chat about and try to steer the conversation toward Robert once in a while."

She nodded dismally.

"By the way, did anything else happen recently in your life

or Rob's? Any deaths in the family? Is he having difficulties in school? Problems at home? Anything like that?"

"Nothing. As you know, he's finishing three years of college in two, and was thinking about his senior thesis."

"Does he have a dissertation topic yet?"

"He's interested in island biogeography."

"What's 'island biogeography'?"

"It's about the fragmentation of the Earth, through development and habitat destruction, into little pieces that are too small for indigenous species to survive."

"Sounds like an interesting topic."

"It is. I might write an article about it myself some time."

"What are you working on now?"

"A piece about some of the new drugs coming out of the rainforests."

"That might fit in well with Rob's studies."

"Yeah," she muttered. "We make a great team."

I took a deep breath and jumped in. "Any problems of a—um—more personal nature?"

"You mean between Rob and me? No, not really. He seems quite happy most of the time."

There was no other way to say this. "Has he been a satisfactory sex partner?"

She blushed slightly and looked away, but I detected a mischievous smile on her face. "More than satisfactory," she assured me. "Why? Did something happen—"

"Just trying to rule out some of the possibilities," I said.

"Well, that's not one of them."

"Giselle . . ." I began. The mischievous smile evaporated. "There's something I have to tell you. Please—sit down."

She complied immediately and waited for me to go on.

I sat down too, and began to drum my pen on the stack of paper covering my desk, a compulsive habit I resort to whenever I need to break unpleasant news and don't know quite where to begin. Finally I told her that I'd spoken with Paul.

She shifted slightly in her chair. "Paul?"

"You remember—the personality who took over whenever Rob found himself in a situation involving—"

"I remember."

"It's possible he's lying, of course, but Paul tells me that it was he and not Rob who is Gene's father."

Her eyes widened, then slowly narrowed. "I know that," she murmured.

"You *know*?"

"At first he had me fooled. I became suspicious when he would start to fall asleep whenever we began to make love, and then he would suddenly be wide awake and very passionate."

"Giselle, why didn't you ever tell me about this?"

"I thought about it. But it was sort of a gradual thing. I wasn't sure until maybe a year ago. And—well, it's hard to explain. I guess I was afraid of what would happen if I did."

"What did you think would happen?"

"I was afraid you'd take him away from me." When I didn't respond, she added, "I knew that Paul was a part of Rob. So at first I thought: What's the difference? Maybe we're all different personalities at different times. You've said the same thing yourself. Rob always came back afterward, and was the same Rob as he was before."

I shook my head a bit and waited.

"Besides, I thought maybe I could help him. Encourage Rob not to be afraid of sex. You know, take it slowly, one step at a time, until he became—well, acclimated to his phobia. Like you do with someone who's afraid of flying or spiders."

"Giselle, you know psychiatry isn't that simple."

She sighed. "You're right. I know that. But I didn't want to lose him. . . ." She was hoping, I suppose, that I would tell her she had done no harm, or at least that I understood.

I did understand. Her motives were partly selfish, partly sympathetic. I felt very sorry for her. But I also felt sorry for Rob, whose problems were infinitely more terrible. "Giselle, is there anything else you want to tell me?"

She pondered this for a moment. "He still misses his father terribly, even thirty-five years after his death. He has a picture of him on the desk in his little study. Once or twice I've heard him talking to it."

"Were you able to hear what he was saying?"

"No, not really. But once I found him crying. It was almost as if he were apologizing to his dad for something."

I knew how he felt. I have often wished that I could apologize to my father for the near-hatred I felt for him when I was a boy and he exerted such a powerful influence on my life, even seeming to have decided what I was going to do with it. It was only later, long after he died, that I realized that whatever happened to me was mostly my own doing. But I'm sure he felt some negative vibes at the time, just as I could tell when my own children resented something I had said or done wrong, however inadvertently.

"One more thing, Giselle. You understand that Paul is a part of Rob. Why not prot, too?"

"Because he told me he isn't!"

No arguing with that. "All right, Giselle, we'll meet again next Tuesday. In the meantime—"

"You'll be the first to know."

After she left I got to thinking about Paul again: how many of the discussions I'd had with Rob two years before were actually with someone else?

SESSION THIRTY-FIVE

I USUALLY spend an hour or two on Thursday morning preparing for my afternoon lecture at Columbia. On this one, however, I found myself thinking about prot's first visit to MPI and how I struggled for weeks trying to determine the underlying basis for his delusion. One of the ideas I wrestled with was that of finding some way to convince him of his earthbound origins. With his impeccable logic, I surmised, this revelation might jolt him to his senses, much as a computer might "crash" after being dealt an impossible problem to solve. At that time, of course, I didn't know about Robert. Once I found him hiding behind prot it became quite a different matter, and I abandoned that strategy in favor of a more direct approach. Now, I realized, the situation had reverted to its original state. If I could prove to prot that he was, in fact, only human, and a mere part of one at that, his whole support structure might collapse and allow me to find Robert's hiding place once more. The danger here was that Rob could be left in the same condition as when prot "departed" in 1990, i.e., an intractable catatonia. On the other hand, if I weren't able to get to Robert before December 31, he would be left exposed and vulnerable anyway. As things stood, there was nothing to lose by taking some calculated risks.

I was encouraged in this endeavor by a paper I had run across a few weeks earlier. In England, in 1950, a man had come to London from an outlying village which, he claimed, was characterized by a matriarchal society. In fact, he had fled his hometown to get away from the "oppressive bitches" who "ruled" there. His therapist discovered that he lived at home with a domineering mother who dictated his every move. When he was confronted by the facts, and established in his own apartment far away from her influence, the delusion quickly dissipated and the man went on to find a wife and, presumably, live happily ever after. It was this sort of logical approach I hoped to use with prot. The only problem was to convince him that the basis for his delusion lay not with a domineering mother, but with the terrible hand fate had dealt his alter ego long before he arrived on the scene.

The lecture did not go well. In fact, it never happened. One of the students had discovered why I had been interrupted by the department chairman the week before and, as soon as I came into the classroom, began to question me about prot. I protested client–patient relationship, but he persisted and was joined by others who wanted to know, in general terms at least, what the current situation was, pointing out that I had written two books about him and that he had appeared on a national television program, so his case was hardly "privileged." I'm a firm believer that teaching is a two-way process, that a professor is usually wise to follow the interests of his students. Thus, the rest of the hour was taken up by my summarizing what had transpired so far, the dilemmas I faced, and what my plans were for dealing with prot/Robert. I had never seen them so animated, so eager to participate. They even forgave me for the pop quiz I had sprung on them earlier.

The aforementioned student, a young man with an enormous black beard (his hero was Oliver Sacks), came up with a quick answer to the whole complex problem: get prot to perform a controlled light-travel demonstration during his next session. "If we can verify this ability," he submitted, "he must be who he says he is."

We? I thought. "He's already done that with a television camera," I retorted. "But you have to remember that he has found a way to use parts of his mind that only autists and savants are able to access. If he 'disappears,' it may mean only that he can trick us into believing it, by a kind of hypnosis or some other means we haven't been able to figure out yet."

"No, no, no," he retorted back. "I mean, get him to go to some specific place—in another part of the country, say—where you've got a colleague waiting to take his photograph. All you have to do is wait for your partner to fax prot's picture to you. You could even have him wear a funny hat or something so there wouldn't be any chance for a mistaken identity."

My expression probably said, Why is there always someone like this in every class? But I responded with, "What if he won't go?"

"Then he can't do it," the student shouted, "and you've got him!" There was a chorus of "Yes!" and "That's right!"

"Might be worth a try," I admitted, wishing I had thought of the idea myself. In a transparent face-saving attempt I added, "But don't bet on it."

When I was finally able to take my leave, "Oliver" and two of his friends followed me out. They all wanted to sit in on my next session with prot. While I was impressed with their obvious interest in the case, I explained the impossibility of complying with their request. The hirsute young man snapped, "All right, keep him to yourself, but we expect a full report next time!"

Great, I thought. Now I could look forward to being grilled before every lecture about prot's progress. As the adage goes, give a medical student enough rope and he'll hang you with it. I was definitely getting too old for this. My wife's unflagging determination that I retire by the summer of '98 was sounding more and more attractive all the time.

When I got back to MPI there was a group of five or six noisy people waiting at the front gate. The security guard had his hands full convincing them that they couldn't go in, that this was a mental hospital, that only the families or friends of the patients could enter, and even then only during visiting hours. When he saw me trying to sneak by his little shed, the guard shouted, "Dr. Brewer, will you talk to these people?"

I swallowed my annoyance; this had not been a good day. "What seems to be the problem?"

One of the group, a woman with fiery red hair and wonderful teeth, responded, "We want to see prot. We know you've got him in there. You have no right to keep him locked up."

I didn't waste any time denying that he was back. "Prot is a patient here. At the moment he's not allowed to have visitors."

A middle-aged man wearing a fatigue jacket and crew cut jumped in front of me. "Why are you keeping him here? He hasn't done anything wrong."

I backed up a step. "We're not 'keeping' him. He volunteered to be here."

He stepped forward. "We don't believe you. That's exactly what you'd say if you were holding him against his will."

I held my ground. "Look, I don't make the rules. What if you had a brother in a hospital and a bunch of people demanded to see him?"

"I'd ask *him* about it!"

"It's not his decision to make."

"Whose decision is it?" another man demanded, his stubbled chin jutting out towards mine.

I backed up again. "Okay, I'll tell you what I'll do. I'll ask prot if he wants to come out and talk to you. If he doesn't, that's the end of it. Fair enough?"

"How do we know you'll ask him?"

"I guess you'll have to trust me on that."

They looked at each other. One or two of them shrugged. "Okay, doc, but we're not leaving until he comes out."

"I probably won't see him until tomorrow."

"What time?"

"Nine o'clock."

"We'll be here at nine."

*   *   *

59

"This is from California, isn't it?" prot opined. "Not as good as the Caribbean mangoes."

"Sorry. Best I could do."

"I'll take it," he slurped. "Clean as a whistle, too," he reported. "Not a trace of any of your so-called pesticides."

I wondered what it looked like to him—vision tests had shown that prot could see well into the ultraviolet range, much like certain insects. "Glad you're enjoying it—it's organic. While you're eating, I'm going to go ahead and ask you a few questions, okay?"

"And if I refuse?"

"No more fruit."

"Ask away."

"How is Robert doing?"

"How should I know?"

"You mean you haven't found him yet?"

"Nope. I looked all over Ward Two and he's nowhere to be found. Besides, I've been pretty busy. . . ."

"Busy? Doing what?"

"Oh, reading my mail, chatting with the other residents, thinking. You remember thinking? You used to do it when you were a boy."

"And Rob hasn't made an appearance since you've been in Ward Two?"

"Nossirree. Maybe he's in one of the other wards."

"It's very important that I speak with him, prot."

"Why? Are you writing another book?"

I pretended not to hear that. "Just let me know right away if you find him, will you? Or tell Giselle."

"W'tever," he grunted, sucking the pulp off the big pit. His beard dripped with mango sludge.

"Good." Unable to stand it any longer, I retrieved a box of facial tissues and handed him one. He wiped off his face, as a courtesy to me, I suppose. Then, annoyingly, he flung the tissue to the floor and settled back in his chair. Frustrated, I exclaimed, "Prot, you're no more from 'K-PAX' than I am. How did you come up with a ridiculous story like that?"

He shook his head. "What does it take to get you humans to see the truth?"

"For one thing, it has to be believable."

"Ah. I remember. If you believe something, it's true, correct?"

"You could put it that way."

"My knowledge of the GALAXY doesn't convince you."

"We have computers that know everything you do."

"Not everything." Suddenly he leaned forward and popped, "What would convince you that I come from K-PAX?" He was obviously eager to play his little game, like a kid with a new chess set.

I thought about the light-travel experiment, but decided to hold it in reserve for the time being. For one thing, I hadn't had a chance to set it up with a partner yet. Instead, I tried another tack. "Do you have any photographs of your home planet?"

"Do you have any photographs of George Washington?"

"No, but we have paintings of him, letters, eyewitness testimony. Do you have any such evidence?"

He looked at me sideways. "I've seen paintings of dragons and unicorns, haven't you? Letters can be forged. And we all know how reliable 'eyewitness testimony' is, don't we, gene?"

"We also have his uniforms, his wigs, even his teeth. What tangible evidence do you have that K-PAX exists, or ever did exist?" I sat back with a smug, prot-like grin.

"What evidence do you have that your gods exist, or ever did exist?"

Exasperated, I shouted, "That's entirely different!"

"Really, gene?"

"Well, there's the Bible, but you probably wouldn't accept that as evidence."

"Who would? Your bibles weren't written by gods, gino. They were written by human beings. You live by rules that were proposed thousands of years ago. At the very least you should revise them every century or so. And what if they got it wrong in the first place?"

"All right. I'm willing to stipulate that *maybe* God didn't write the Bible, and even that *maybe* there are no gods at all, if you'll agree that *maybe* K-PAX never existed either."

"One problem."

"What's that?"

"I've been there!"

"So you're asking me to take K-PAX on faith?"

He didn't miss a beat. "Not at all. You can come with me if you want. See for yourself. I've still got room for one or two more."

There was no good response to this preposterous suggestion. But, I wondered, could religion be a more important part of Rob's dilemma than I had thought? I decided to pursue this. "Most of our religions tell us that if we have enough faith, we'll end up in heaven."

"Religions aren't a question of 'faith.' They're a matter of indoctrination."

"That doesn't prove they're wrong. Anyway, right or wrong, if religions do us good, make us feel better—"

"They do seem rather benign, don't they, my illogical friend? The fact is, they are one of your most dangerous aberrations."

"Aberrations?"

"Religions are a cop-out. They free you from taking the responsibility for your own actions."

"But surely we need to have an ethical foundation of some kind. Without moral laws, what motive would we have to behave?"

He chuckled a little, obviously enjoying himself. "You don't behave anyway, despite your thousands of religions!"

"How easy for you 'K-PAXians' not to need any help with your lives. There's no cruelty, no injustice, no evil of any kind on your planet, is there?"

"'Evil' is a purely human concept. It exists only on EARTH. And a few other class B PLANETS."

This session, like yesterday's lecture, wasn't going quite as planned. Instead of me putting him on the spot, it was prot who had taken charge, as usual. Furthermore, I was distracted by the soiled tissue he had thrown on the floor. "Let me think about that."

"You won't regret it, believe me. And as for your gods," he added cheerfully, "maybe you're right. Maybe there's a heaven and maybe there's a hell. Anything's possible in this crazy UNIVERSE."

I had an odd feeling I had been checkmated again. I tried the more direct approach. "You know Robert pretty well. Tell me: do you think religion might have had some kind of deleterious effect on his mind?"

"I wouldn't be at all surprised. It has that effect on most of you. Wracked by doubt if you believe there's a god, torn by fear if you don't." He shook his head. "Horrible! But you'll have to ask him that for yourself. We never talked about it. Except for his wife's being a catholic."

"Did that bother him a lot?"

"No, but it bothered a lot of his so-called friends, most of whom he'd known since childhood. Go figure."

Ordinarily I would have pursued the matter of Robert's childhood friends. But this was no ordinary case, and there wasn't enough time to peer into every dark corner. "Tell me something about your own childhood on K-PAX."

He quickly produced his trademark grin and asked me what I'd like to know.

I went for the jugular. "Why don't we start at the beginning? What's the earliest thing you can remember?"

"I can remember the womb," he mused.

"What?" I sat up a little straighter. "What was it like?"

"It was nice and warm."

"About like K-PAX on a nice, sunny day?"

"It's always sunny on K-PAX."

"Of course. I had forgotten. What else do you remember about the womb?"

"There wasn't much room to move around."

"So I've heard. But it was comfortable, otherwise?"

"I suppose so. Noisy, though. A lot of pounding and gurgling."

"Your mother's heart. Stomach. Intestines."

"I could hear her lungs, too. Wheeze, wheeze, wheeze."

"You realized even before you were born what was causing all that racket?"

"Not really. Not in words, anyway."

"Okay, you remember the womb. Does this mean you remember being born?"

"Yep. What a hassle."

"In what way?"

"It's a pretty tight squeeze, coach."

"Did it hurt?"

"I had a headache for days. *Your* days, I mean."

"Of course. So you didn't much like being in the womb, and being born wasn't too agreeable an experience, either. What about when you found yourself out in the world—was that as unpleasant as all the rest?"

"Some of the smells weren't too savory."

"Like what?"

"Now, gene, are you telling me you haven't noticed that poo-poo happens?"

"Now that you mention it, I have on occasion. Do babies wear diapers on K-PAX, or what?"

"It's not cold there. They don't wear anything."

"Babies run around naked on your planet?"

"Naturally. They do on this PLANET, too. In the summer, anyway."

"So you were exposed to the elements, and to your relatives and anyone else who happened to be around. Is that right?"

"None of my relatives were there, as far as I know."

"Not even your mother?"

"Only for a little while."

"How about one of your uncles?"

"Huh?"

"Did you have any uncles hanging around?"

"I already answered that."

"Meaning you don't know for sure."

"Nope."

"Okay—you say your father abandoned your mother after you were born?"

"No, he left *before* I was born. Where I come from, no father hovers around waiting for a child to show up. It's no big deal."

"If I remember correctly, you said you've never even met your father, is that right?"

"No, I said that if we have met, our biological connection wasn't pointed out to me."

"K-PAXian fathers leave their children to fend for themselves, is that it?"

"Of course. Mothers do, too. We don't have parents to brainwash us, like you do on EARTH."

"Who does brainwash you?"

"No one does. Children are free to learn what they want, pursue whatever interests them."

"Without any kind of supervision whatever?"

"Only enough to make sure they don't harm themselves in some way."

"Who does the supervising?"

"Gene, gene, gene. We went over this years ago!"

"Refresh my memory. Who makes sure your children don't get themselves into trouble?"

"Whoever happens to be around."

"What if no one is around?"

"There is always someone around to do what needs to be done."

"An uncle, for example?"

Prot was becoming a trifle annoyed. "I wouldn't know

my uncle from a lorgon" (a goatlike creature found on
K-PAX).

"Well, did *anyone* bother you in any way after you were
born?"

"Not that I recall."

"Would you remember if someone did?"

"Of course."

"Are you sure?"

"You should get your hearing aid checked, gino."

Another feeble attempt at K-PAXian humor, I suppose.
But it also meant that prot was becoming testier, which was
exactly what I wanted. "All right. Who bathed you when you
were a baby?"

He slapped his forehead. "In the first place, babies don't
take baths on K-PAX—there's no water, remember? In the
second place, we're not obsessed with every speck of dust on
our skins, as you humans seem to be. And in the third place,
if I needed to be cleaned, someone would do it."

"How were you cleaned when you were a baby?"

"I was wiped off with fallid leaves. They're soft and moist."

"Who did that for you?"

"Whoever was around."

"Your mother?"

"If she was around."

"In other words, a baby is at the mercy of 'whoever is
around'?"

"Spoken like a true homo sapiens."

"That's because no one would ever harm another being on
K-PAX, right?"

"Now you're getting it."

"Did one of your uncles hang around the house a lot?"

He whacked his forehead again. "We don't have houses on K-PAX."

"Well, did one of them hang around your neighborhood, or wherever it was you lived?"

"What is this obsession you have with uncles?" he screeched. "We don't have uncles! We don't know anything about uncles! Do you understand?"

"Do you resent the question?"

"I resent stupidity!"

"All right. I think that's enough for one session, don't you?"

"Plenty!" he said, jumping up and heading for the door. He still had an orange ring around his mouth.

"See you Tuesday!" I called out.

The only reply was the door being slammed.

After disposing of the soiled facial tissue I listened to the tape of our conversation. It was curiously satisfying to hear him become agitated at the mention of nudity, of bathing, of putative uncles. Was baby Robin harmed in some way by someone "who happened to be around"? There was a definite sore spot being touched here, and I was pretty sure we were on the right track. The only question was, did it lead to a brick wall?

Then there was prot's abhorrence of religions, or perhaps the concept of 'faith' in general. Was Robert betrayed by someone he had faith in? Perhaps even a clergyman? I made a note to ask Giselle what she knew about his religious background.

In my office I found a message from the head of security—the people gathered on the sidewalk outside the front gate were demanding to speak with prot. I had forgotten all about them. Perhaps I subconsciously hoped they would just go away. I got the guy on the phone. "Find Giselle," I told him, "and get her to take care of it."

Early that afternoon I received a call from a colleague now living in Germany, though he is an American and went to medical school in the United States. In fact, we interned together at Bellevue. Though an incorrigible practical joker, he is a brilliant psychoanalyst and extremely personable as well. After chatting for a bit about our respective families he told me he had a patient in his hospital claiming to be from the planet K-PAX. "You've opened a can of worms," he cheerfully informed me. "Now there are going to be 'prots' popping up all over the place. As a matter of fact, there's another one I've heard about in China, and one in Congo, of all places."

"This isn't like your horse joke, is it?"

"Gene! Would I do that to you?"

"Yes! You did, in fact!"

"Well, maybe I did. But this involves a patient."

"All right, what's your guy like?" I asked him.

"Much like the man you've described in your books. But he calls himself 'char,' pronounced 'care.'"

"Does he like fruit?"

"Can't get enough of it."

"Can he draw star maps from various places around the galaxy?"

"No, he has another talent."

"What's that?"

"He claims he has a direct pipeline to God."

"Did you test him on that?"

"I asked him if there's really a heaven."

"And is there?"

"Yes. But there's a catch."

"What's that?"

"There aren't any people there."

"Sounds like a genuine K-PAXian to me."

"Who knows?"

"That reminds me, George. I wonder if you'd do me a favor."

"Sure."

"Do you have a camera?"

"Is the Pope Catholic? Is grass green? Do skunks—"

"Okay, okay. Here's what I'm going to do. I'm going to send *our* K-PAXian to see you. I mean, don't hold your breath, but just in case he shows up, would you get a picture of him and fax it to me right away?"

"When's he coming?"

"How about next Tuesday? At 9:15 A.M., say, which would be—what—3:15 there?"

"I'll be out front waiting for him. Does he have the address?"

"No, but I'll give it to him. Got to run. Thanks for calling, Herr Doktor. And take care of *your* K-PAXian."

"Any suggestions as to how?"

"I was hoping you'd tell *me*!"

As soon as I hung up, I realized I was already a few minutes late for my next patient, an obsessive-compulsive who must go through one or another endless ritual before he can perform the simplest act. For example, he can't eat until he has washed his hands and face exactly thirty-two times. If he loses count he has to start over. And if he touches anything on the way to the dining room he must find a washroom and go through the whole procedure again.

But Linus's difficulties go well beyond this. A biochemist with two doctoral degrees, he was part of a team trying to map the human genome, the complete chemical sequence of the DNA strands comprising each of our forty-six chromosomes, a formidable task requiring hundreds of scientists and all the latest technology.

His problems began to surface almost as soon as he was assigned to work on the project. In his first paper (with about fifteen co-authors), one of the referees noticed some peculiarities in the sequencing of the gene which governs how we taste sourness. On careful examination, it seemed that the section of DNA Linus had worked on was identical to part of another gene, except the forty or so components had been reversed. Someone was asked to check his data, but his notebooks had somehow been misplaced or stolen, and the experiments could not be repeated by other members of the laboratory.

At this point his thesis work came under closer scrutiny and it was discovered that none of that was verifiable either, and those original notes and data had disappeared also. To make a long and gruesome story short, our Linus knew nothing about biochemistry whatever, or much of anything else. How had he obtained his Ph.D.'s? No one knows, but it must have been a remarkable con job. (It was reported that his graduate-school seminars were so complex that no one could understand them, which presumably only enhanced his reputation as a brilliant researcher.)

A mild form of compulsive behavior was noted during his student days, but it was during the genome studies that he began to suffer from obsessive compulsions of a very serious nature. He sharpened dozens of pencils every morning before he could start to work. From this he rapidly progressed to a daily cleaning of the office he shared with a fellow biochemist. But it was when he began tidying up his *partner's* desk, and, finally, shining every piece of glassware in the laboratory before he could get going, that he was put on temporary leave and encouraged to find help.

Why would someone so patently brilliant as Linus (his IQ approaches 180) falsify his research and try to make a career out of gibberish when it would have been easier just to do the experiments honestly and report the actual results?

Obsessive-compulsive disorder is an age-old affliction closely related to certain other anxiety disorders, and often grounded in anal fixation. Monoamine oxidase inhibitors and certain tricyclics have proven beneficial in a limited number of cases, as has cingulatomy, a surgical procedure. Psychoanalysis has not been very effective, however, perhaps because free association merely increases the level of fixation on a particular obsession. The best and most common approach is to expose the patient to whatever triggers the compulsive behavior, prevent his engaging in the usual rituals, and confront the underlying anxiety.

Sometimes OCD covers up a severe inferiority complex. Linus's father is a well-known chemist, and his mother a highly regarded mycologist and one of the world's foremost experts on poisonous mushrooms. Had he tried to live up to their expectations, an elusive goal shared by many highly successful people in all sorts of endeavors? Or had some specific event precipitated his abnormal behavior?

I welcomed him into my examining room for our bimonthly session. Naturally he declined my offer of prot's leftover fruit. "Didn't wash your hands before you came up?"

Linus, who is not especially handsome in any case, screwed up his face. "No. I just don't like fruit."

"Otherwise it doesn't bother you to eat it?"

"Not particularly."

"You're a scientist," I reminded him. "Let's do an experiment."

He looked horrified. "I—I can't."

"What do you think would happen if you ate it?"

He squeaked, "I have to go wash my hands!"

"Try a bite of mango first. I assure you it's clean. Prot said so."

He stopped wringing his hands. "He said that?" I thought for a moment I was going to witness one of prot's wondrous cures. Obviously struggling to make a decision, Linus stared intensely at the fruit. But suddenly he backed away from it as if it were a gun. "Please!" he begged. "Let me go wash my hands first!" He hurried away to scrub off any contamination he may have encountered by being in the same room with me and an overripe mango. I didn't try to stop him. In fact, it occurred to me, as it has to every other member of the staff, to turn him over to prot and see what *he* could do with him.

*   *   *

Over my wife's protestations I drove to the hospital early on Saturday morning. She thought we should go looking for a retirement home.

"I'm not retired yet!" I pointed out.

"It's just a matter of time!" she parried.

"We'll talk about that after prot leaves. Until then, I don't want to think about it."

She accepted that, I guess. After all, December 31 wasn't very far off.

On weekdays I usually take the train and come in the back way, but, since I had driven down, I parked in the garage around the corner and entered through the front gate. To my surprise, and no little annoyance, I found that the half-dozen or so people gathered around it had become a crowd of forty or fifty. I tried to slip through, but someone recognized me and demanded that I "let prot go."

"He can go any time he wants," I calmly reminded him.

"Then why are there guards at the gate?"

"We have some dangerous individuals here. I don't think you'd want to see them on the streets."

A few of the patients were milling about the grounds. "They don't look very dangerous," someone else observed.

"Not them. But there are others . . ."

"Is prot dangerous?"

"Not a bit."

"Then why don't you let him go?"

"I told you—he can go any time he wants! In fact, he's leaving on New Year's Eve!" While the crowd digested this news I sidled past the guard and hurried up the walk to the front door of the hospital wondering why Giselle hadn't taken care of this nagging problem, and noting as I did so that time

74

had stopped again for the crew working on the new wing. It occurred to me that Albert's problem might be solved by putting him in charge of the building committee.

As soon as I got inside I called Giselle's apartment. Her mother told me she wasn't home, adding, "I hope you can find Rob soon. We all miss him."

I called the nurses' station on Ward Two and she wasn't there, either. Still annoyed, I rounded up all the original notes in prot's file and began to go over them, looking hard for clues and inconsistencies. There *had* to be something I had overlooked before and was overlooking now. The only things I came up with were some questions about Rob's dog, Apple, who was run over and killed when Robin was nine, and the recollection that his Uncle Dave and Aunt Catherine died in a fire soon afterward. Were these two events related in some way?

Frustrated and disappointed, I decided to have lunch in Ward Three, the home of the sexual and social deviates and certain other unfortunates. As always, I was amazed how eating seems to counteract the symptoms of most mental illnesses, if only temporarily. In fact, during that brief period it was difficult to tell the autists from the coprophilics, and I wondered whether some use could be made of this observation: i.e., whether pleasurable sensations of one sort might be useful in the treatment of problems of a different sort. Would stimulating certain areas of the brain, for example, be a way of alleviating the intensity of other, less desirable, sensations? Would marijuana or cocaine overcome the unpleasantness of OCD or bipolar disorder? This reminded me of the early attempts to cure syphilis by infecting patients with malaria. The comparison seemed apt. Psychiatry is at about the same stage now as internal medicine was a century ago.

I sat across from Jerry and Lenny, two of our autistic patients, remembering the day more than two years earlier when prot had awakened Jerry from his "dream" world long enough for the latter to communicate certain thoughts and feelings he had long bottled up inside. How had prot done that? Unfortunately, this was another conundrum that would probably have to wait for future generations to solve.

As for the present, I could almost feel a certain amount of tension around the table, which was considerably quieter than usual, hardly any spitting or wailing at all. But it wasn't until everyone had finished eating (except for those who sculpt their food into birds or squish it into a homogeneous mess before starting) that one of the incurable voyeurs, sitting at the other end of the table, politely asked if prot could come to lunch next time. Total silence descended immediately, like a black curtain. Jerry and Lenny weren't exactly looking at me, but they weren't ogling the walls and ceilings, either. What could I say? I told my luncheon companions I would extend the invitation right away. The room broke into spontaneous happy laughter that went on and on. It was quite infectious. Everyone looked at everyone else and laughed even harder. I don't remember when I'd had such a good time, though I'm still not sure what we were laughing about.

That afternoon I listened to tapes of some of my early conversations with prot (and, less frequently, with Robert), marveling yet again at his ultraconfidence in the truth of his bizarre confabulation. A world of his own creation that was unbelievably perfect, so carefully thought out as to be seamless and, yes, almost convincing. If we could all focus our attention to such a degree on any worthwhile project, he had often reminded me, who knows what we might accomplish.

I think I dozed off for a minute and was awakened by the phone. It was Giselle "reporting in." "You looking for me, Dr. B?"

"Huh? Oh yes. Those people hanging around the front gate—have you spoken to them yet?"

"Yes, I have. They won't leave until they see prot."

"Can't you get rid of them?"

"Not until he makes an appearance."

"This is turning into a circus."

"Maybe Milton could put on his clown suit and warm them up with his juggling act."

"Get serious, Giselle. If word gets out, the media will have a field day with this."

"You worry too much, boss. Let me take care of it for you. That's why I'm here, remember?"

"Make it soon."

After some shuffling and filing I listened to a few more tapes, and it wasn't until late afternoon that I grabbed up all the ones I hadn't yet heard and headed for the parking lot. The crowd was still out front and was, if anything, larger. This problem, like all those connected with prot's "visit," just wasn't going to go away. I turned around and left by the back door.

Karen and I had tickets to the Met's lavish presentation of *Turandot* for that Saturday evening, and I looked forward to a night of relaxation and enjoyment. But this particular opera is about riddles and answers, and my thoughts came right back to prot and the unanswered questions: Why had Robert withdrawn so abruptly, how could we get him back, and what would happen to him when prot made his year-end "departure," this time for good? With the New Year looming like a guillotine, there was more urgency than ever to get to the bottom of things. But a personal note had also crept into my thinking. If I could solve this puzzle, the case of Robert/prot would be an accomplishment worthy of ending a career. If not, I would be quitting a loser.

I was encouraged, though, by a tremendous round of cheers and applause, and I took a bow, not quite knowing why. The next thing I knew Karen was elbowing me, whispering that the opera was over. "If you were going to doze through the whole thing," she added, "we could have stayed home and watched a movie on TV. You could have slept better there."

SESSION THIRTY-SIX

Monday was one of those days when, for some reason, I felt discombobulated, as if I were on the outside looking in. I wasn't pleased with what I saw.

There was something about prot, something all-consuming, that made everything else seem unimportant by comparison. All of my "free" time seemed to go into his (Robert's) case. When I wasn't studying my notes or listening to the tapes, I was thinking about them.

Some of the other staff members were beginning to slide down this slippery slope as well. During the regular Monday meeting most of them were astonished by the revelation that prot seemed able to remember being born, and even lying in the womb. Some, especially Thorstein, saw this as a golden opportunity, suggesting I spend several more sessions pinning down the earliest moment prot could recall.

Our newest young psychiatrist, Laura Chang, agreed. She herself wanted to "pick his brain," after hours if necessary, pointing out that perhaps the root of many mental difficulties lay in the very earliest moments of our experience. It is her view, in fact, that certain formative patterns might be initiated in the late-stage embryo, who must be quite mystified indeed by all the harsh sounds he hears, the strange smells and tastes he may be aware of, assuming, of course, that he is conscious (her hypothesis) at times. I could understand their motives, having stated in the past that much could be learned from prot's apparent depth of knowledge about many esoteric subjects, whatever its nature. I reminded everyone yet again that our responsibility was to Robert, not to prot, and that this should be the basis for any protocol.

The meeting ended with a discussion of the upcoming outing, for those patients who wanted, and were able, to visit the Metropolitan Museum of Art, and notice of a long-overdue visit by the popular psychologist known to the public as "America's TV shrink," who had abruptly cancelled a similar trip two years earlier for personal reasons.

Afterward, I invited Goldfarb for coffee in the doctors' dining room, intending to speak with her about the crowd of people hanging around the gate. But she had her own agenda, high on the list of which was an attempt to schedule formal interviews between prot and some of her patients. I peered into those thick glasses, behind which her eyes looked like pinpoints, and tried to change the subject back to the circus going on out front. But she had no interest in dealing with it unless there were some disturbance or other. I pointed out that they were her responsibility. She accepted this and went over to refill her cup. I have never known anyone who could drink hot coffee as fast as Goldfarb.

The other reason I had wanted to speak with her was to talk

her into allowing me temporary leave from some of my duties, particularly those of an optional or peripheral nature, such as the various hospital and university committees I served on and, especially, chairing the one overseeing the completion, if ever, of the new wing. I even tried to foist off a few of my most difficult patients (Frankie and Linus) on her or another colleague, and blatantly inquired about the possibility of someone taking over my lecture course. Hoping this would be the coup d'état, I added, "I'm thinking of retiring next summer."

Goldfarb broke into a nasal giggle. She drained her steaming cup, got up and strode out, still chuckling. As she left I heard her whinny, "You'll never retire!"

On my way out to give my afternoon lecture at Columbia, I ran into Giselle. "Isn't it great?" she chirped.

"Huh? What do you mean?"

"Like they said, all they wanted was to talk to prot."

"Who? Oh, you mean the people—Well, is he going to—"

"He already did."

"What? He talked to them?"

"Yesterday."

"I see. And what did he tell them?"

"He said he didn't have room for them all on this trip."

"You mean they all want to go with him?"

"Not all. But some of them did."

"What was their reaction to being left behind?"

"They asked him to come back for them!"

"And is he going to do that?"

"Nope."

"Why not?"

"He's already said he's never coming back, remember?"

"What did they think about that?"

"Not much until he told them someone else might do it."
She waited, her brown eyes twinkling like a cat that had just
finished a canary.

"Well, when is the next K-PAXian due to come for them?"

"He couldn't say. In fact, he couldn't guarantee that anyone
from K-PAX would ever visit the Earth again."

"Didn't this make things worse?"

"Not when he told them we already have K-PAX here. He
says the Earth could be just like K-PAX if we wanted
it badly enough. Nobody said anything for a while, until a
twelve- or thirteen-year-old boy asked him, 'How do we do
that?'" She paused again in her mischievous way.

Milton slouched by, grumbling, "Hemorrhoids are a pain
in the ass. . . ."

I asked her impatiently, "Okay, I'm curious. What was the
answer?"

"He said, 'That's up to you.'"

"That's what I figured he'd say."

"And then he went back in."

"So why are they still here?"

"They're not. But it doesn't make any difference."

"Why not?"

"Because they were soon replaced by another group. *They*
wanted to speak with prot, too."

"God, is there no end to this?"

"These people aren't crazy, Dr. B. You should go out and
talk to them some time. There are plumbers, housewives,
accountants, factory workers and—well, you name it. I'd
write an article about them if there were time."

"Why isn't there time?"

"If prot takes Rob with him, I expect to go, too."

"To K-PAX."

"That's right."

"Don't you know for sure?"

She looked as if she'd been shot. "Not exactly. I guess I'd better ask him about that."

"What if prot doesn't find Rob? Then you'll stay behind with *him*, correct?"

"He'll find him!"

"One more thing: Don't let him talk to anybody from the media. We've got enough trouble without that."

"Easier said than done!"

The afternoon lecture went surprisingly well. When I told the students that a colleague in Germany was prepared to receive prot at 9:15 in the morning, "Oliver Sacks" volunteered to organize a "surveillance committee" to man every entrance to the hospital and monitor prot's possible comings and goings.

Another can of worms. Inasmuch as there was nothing to lose, however, I agreed. "But be discreet. I don't want anyone hanging around before nine or after ten o'clock. And you have to stay outside the wards. Fair enough?"

This seemed to satisfy everyone concerned, and I went on with the lecture, which, as I suspected, was one of the most muddled I ever presented. Nonetheless, the students gave me their rapt attention and, except for the scratching of pens on paper, were supremely attentive. Or perhaps they were merely mulling over prot's possible origins, as was I.

In fact, it was sometime during the presentation that a chilling thought popped into my head: *How did prot's boyhood on K-PAX compare with his alter ego's tragic life here on Earth?*

I came prepared for my next session with prot, having listened by then to all of the tapes of our earlier meetings, re-read his "report," and watched the video of his television appearance. There was no way I was going to allow him to sidetrack the interview with his superior memory and quibbling about small details. In fact, I decided to emphasize the seriousness of the hour by forgoing the fruit.

"That's the main reason I'm here!" he wailed. He sat facing me glumly, his Cheshire-cat grin only a memory. It occurred to me that maybe he was putting me on.

I started the tape recorder. "Did you find Rob?"

"Checked every closet and behind every tree. He's nowhere to be found. Maybe he went back to Guelph."

"How would he get out without anyone noticing him?"

"Maybe he never came in."

I nodded pleasantly. "Prot, I have a colleague in Germany who wants to see you for a moment." I handed him a slip of paper. "Here's the address."

Prot studied the information. "I'll try to squeeze it in."

"No—you don't understand. He wants to see you *now*. At 9:15 this morning."

"Your sense of humour still needs work gino. I've already performed this stunt for you. Even if I did it again you'd never believe it. You'd think it was some kind of trick."

"No I wouldn't! This would be the proof we need that you're really who you say you are!"

"How many times do I have to prove it?"

"Just this once."

"Sorry. No can do."

"Why the hell not?"

"I told you already. Besides, what if Robert shows up while I'm gone?"

"But Dr. Ehrhart is waiting!"

"Has he nothing else to do?"

"He has plenty to do!"

"So do I!"

"So you refuse to cooperate."

"I'm here, ain't I?"

Even though I knew he couldn't zip off to Germany or anywhere else, I had rarely been angrier in a session with a patient of mine. "Prot," I screeched, "why don't you just admit it? You can't do it, can you?"

"Of course I can."

"You're not from K-PAX, are you? You're a fake and a phony! Everyone knows it!"

"Surely not everyone."

"It's because of the fruit, isn't it?"

"Nope. We're not a petty, vindictive species like some others I could name."

"A lot of people are going to be disappointed."

"Won't be the last time."

I stared at him for a while to emphasize my displeasure. "Dr. Ehrhart claims that other 'K-PAXians' are popping up around the world."

"Could be. Or maybe they're lunatics."

Grabbing a yellow pad, I said, rather petulantly, I'm sure, "All right, damn it, tell me more about your phony boyhood."

"You never get enough, do you, doc?"

"I may make an exception in your case."

"No you won't. You're bound and determined to pry every little secret from everyone here."

"That's what psychiatrists are for."

"That so? I thought they were for making piles of money to 'feed their families,' like every other sapiens in this god-forsaken place" (he meant the Earth).

Recalling that Robert's family had been exceptionally poor, I asked him, "You don't like the capitalist system very much, do you, prot?"

"Frankly, my dear, it sucks."

"What's wrong with it? It's worked pretty well throughout our history."

"Then why do you have so many problems?"

"Look. If there were no trading or bartering, no legal tender, everyone would have to grow his own food, make his own clothes, produce his own transportation, and all the rest. A terrible waste of time and energy, wouldn't you say?"

"At last I understand what's wrong with you—you're all nuts!"

"No need for insults, prot, or whoever you are."

"Merely an observation, my thin-skinned friend. None of you seems to have the ability to see a bigger picture, to figure out the consequences of your actions, or even to look at a problem rationally. You're a bunch of wild-eyed schizo-phrenics!"

"What problem?" I calmly asked him.

"And on top of that, you can't follow a conversation. Look. You've given me the pros of the money system. Have you given any thought to the cons?"

"I suppose you're talking about the way some people abuse it."

"That's a start."

"Well, I suppose it must seem unfair to the disadvantaged."

"Keep going. . . ."

"I don't know what you're getting at."

"Do you ever listen to the evening news? Read a newspaper?"

"Sometimes."

"What's the result of all that brainwashing?"

"Brainwashing?"

He tapped his fingers together and looked up at the ceiling.

"What's the result of all the focus on the 'economy,' on 'jobs,' on 'growth,' on—"

"But everyone benefits when—"

"Really, gene? Do *all* your beings benefit? Do the elephants and tigers benefit? Does your PLANET benefit?"

"You're repeating yourself. That's exactly what you said on TV two years ago."

"And you didn't hear it then, either!"

"But everyone is already aware of the environment. We all know about global warming. Scientists in every country are studying the problem—"

Prot guffawed. "When are you humans going to stop 'studying' your problems and start *doing* something about them?"

"We *are* doing something about this one! We're trying to reduce greenhouse gases to 1990 levels, for example."

"Har har har—you people kill me! It's 1990 levels that are causing the problem!"

"You don't understand. We have to balance one benefit against another. We have to compro—"

"Compromising on your environment is like removing half a tumor."

"It's not that simple, prot. Jobs are at stake. Lives are at stake."

"Exactly."

"What's that supposed to mean?"

"You're trapped in a quagmire of money and you can't seem to find a way out of it. In the meantime, your PLANET is dying. And the really nutty thing about it is that you hardly even notice. Catastrophe is right around the corner, and when you get there you'll all wring your hands and pretend you didn't see it coming."

"And how much time do you figure we have left, exactly?"

"Twenty-three years," he said matter-of-factly.

"You mean our species has only twenty-three years left on Earth?"

"Did I say that, doc? I mean that if the necessary changes aren't made by that time, certain events will be set in motion and then there will be no stopping the slide."

"And how did you arrive at that figure?"

"I didn't. It was worked out by another K-PAXian."

"Based on what?"

"She used the data from my report. It's simple. You can do it yourself. All you need is a primitive computer. . . ."

"If it's so simple, why didn't *you* work it out?"

"Same reason you didn't—I don't give a damn what happens to your murderous, self-centered species. What saddens me is that you're taking all the other beings with you."

"I give a damn!"

"Then why haven't you worked it out?"

"Look, prot, maybe you're right," I said to mollify him. "But it's time to get on with our session, okay?"

"Sure," he shrugged. "Why not? It's not my problem, anyway."

"Because you'll be leaving us soon."

"Righto."

"Back to K-PAX, where there *are* no problems."

"Exactly."

"Tell me more about your boyhood there. Were you poor?"

"No one is 'poor' on K-PAX! Or rich, either. It's a meaningless concept."

"Tell me what your early childhood was like."

He stared at the empty fruit bowl. Finally he said, "Okay—how early is early?"

"Oh, up to the age of six, say."

"*Your* years, of course."

"Or the K-PAXian equivalent."

"To tell you everything would take me about six years, wouldn't it? You got that much time, gino?"

"Dammit, prot, just give me the highlights."

"The whole thing was a highlight. Wasn't yours?"

I sighed. "All right. Let's say you're five. In Earth terms, of course. It's your fifth birthday today. Is there a party for you? A birthday cake?"

"None of the above."

"Why not?"

"We don't have cakes on K-PAX. Or parties. Or birthdays."

"No birthdays?"

"Our annual cycles vary a bit depending on—well, I don't suppose you want to go into the ASTRONOMICAL details."

"Not just now."

"I didn't think so. In any case, nobody cares when someone was born or how old he is. It's completely irrelevant."

"What about friends? Are they irrelevant, too?"

"You need to re-read your own books. Everyone on K-PAX is a 'friend.' We don't have 'enemies.' We just don't need them, as you seem to."

"Naturally. Pets?"

"Certainly not."

"Toys? Games?"

"Not the kind you mean."

"What kind is that?"

"We don't have 'monopoly' to teach us the value of making money. Or toy soldiers to teach us the importance of the military. Or dolls to teach us the joys of parenthood. None of that crap." He thought a moment. "Besides, all of life is a game. On K-PAX life is fun. Right from the start."

"Nary a problem, is that right?"

"Only little ones, but even those are fun."

"What sorts of little fun problems did you have to deal with?"

"Oh, you know—scrapes and bruises, an occasional stomach ache, that sort of thing."

"Those don't sound like much fun to me."

"It's a part of life, don'tcha know."

"Ever get into a fight with one of your 'friends'?"

"No one fights on K-PAX."

"So how do you get the scrapes and bruises? Does someone punish you for behaving badly?"

"No one behaves badly. What's the point? And if we did, there would be no punishment."

"But someone gave you the bruises, didn't they?"

"Didn't you ever fall out of a tree, my human friend?"

"Once or twice. You never had an abusive uncle, anything like that?"

"Where do you get this 'uncle' shit? I told you—I don't know from 'uncle'!"

"All right. Anyone else bother you when you were a small boy? A passerby, perhaps?"

"Of course not!"

"Okay—what sorts of things did you do when you were little?"

"I watched the korms [birds], ran with the aps [small, elephant-like creatures]. I learned the names of the fruits and grains, studied the stars, traveled around, spent some time in the libraries, ate, slept—you know: I did whatever needed to be done and, after that, whatever I felt like doing."

"Did you have a bicycle? Roller skates?"

"Nah. Who needs those things?"

"You just walked wherever you wanted to go?"

"It's a good way to get around, and you see more than you do going by light."

"What about that? I mean, when did you first experience light travel?"

"Right away. Of course I rode along with someone else until I figured out how to do it."

"When you were five?"

"Long before that."

"Who did you ride with?"

"Whoever was around."

"Of course. And who were you staying with when you were five years old?"

He slapped his forehead. "No one 'stays' with anyone on K-PAX. We like to move around."

"Why is that?"

"K-PAX is a big place. There's a lot to see." (Unlike tiny Guelph, Montana.)

"Did anyone you knew die when you were six?"

That shot flew over his head, apparently. "Probably an ancient fart or two. Hardly anyone ever dies on K-PAX."

"So you've told me. All right, prot. Our time is up for today. You can go now. I'll see you on Friday."

He jumped up and jogged to the door. "Don't take any wooden nickels!" he shouted on his way out.

I assumed he was putting me on again.

George must have thought the "light-travel" experiment had been a great joke. When I returned to my inner office I found a fax from him with a picture of a very old horse, ribs showing, head hanging down. An arrow identified the bony critter as "prot." I thought about calling him to explain the situation, but just then Giselle showed up. She seemed in much better spirits than she had for some time. When I mentioned this obvious change, she exclaimed that if prot found Rob and took him to K-PAX, she would definitely get to go along, too!

"He told you that?"

"Yep!"

"My godson going, too?"

"Yep!"

"Then I guess you'd better help him find Rob, right?"

The smile vanished. "How can I do that?"

I asked her to start by filling in any missing details she might have about Rob's background, things she might have learned in her two years of sitting at the breakfast table with him, watching movies, making plans over a glass of wine, and all the other occasions which contribute to a happy and intimate relationship. Unfortunately, she didn't know much more about him than I did. They rarely discussed his childhood—it was painful for him (and for her as well)—or his previous marriage (for the same reasons). However, she did tell me a couple of surprising things about his likes and dislikes. For example, although he was interested in most scientific subjects, including field biology, the focus of his academic studies, he actually disliked astronomy. He wouldn't even watch reruns of the old *Star Trek* series or the myriad spin-offs. Another peculiar characteristic was his abhorrence of bathtubs. He took showers exclusively, and wouldn't even enter the bathroom when she was in the tub.

I thought: Did something happen while little Robin was taking a bath? "Anything else you can think of?"

"Nothing out of the ordinary."

"Any religious beliefs?"

"Rob isn't an atheist, but he's not very religious, either. More of an agnostic, I suppose."

"Did he ever tell you about his toy soldiers, discuss the war in Vietnam, anything like that?"

"He has toy soldiers?"

"When he was a boy he did."

"So did my brothers and everybody else I know."

"Did he ever rail about being poor when he was growing up, or profess any negative feelings about the free-enterprise system? Or what it might be doing to the environment?"

"He's a biologist, Dr. B. Of course he talks about the degradation of the environment. But he has never showed any communist leanings, anything like that, if that's what you mean."

"Does he think the Earth is going to hell in a handbag?"

"No more than anyone else. Why? Did prot tell you Rob had radical ideas on all these things?"

"Not exactly. I'm still trying to get a handle on Rob's problems. Do me a favor, Giselle. Will you think about this some more, and when we meet again could you give me a report on anything unusual that might come to mind about Rob's behavior the past couple of years? And make me a complete list of his likes and dislikes, particularly any strong ones. Will you do that?"

She blinked those big, doelike eyes. "Sure, if you think it will help."

I chose not to divulge my misgivings about that.

As I was passing through the lounge I encountered Frankie sitting in her customary place on the wide windowsill staring at the lawn. I asked her why she didn't get her coat on and go outside for a walk. She replied, characteristically, "It's shitty out there."

"Frankie, it's a beautiful day!"

"Beauty is in the eye of the beholder," she scowled. "Or so they say. I wouldn't know—I've never encountered it."

"Don't you think the sunshine is beautiful? The green grass, especially in late November? The leaves blowing in the wind?"

"What's so beautiful about death and decay?" She stared at my left cheek. "That's the ugliest mole I've ever seen."

"Isn't there *anything* you think is beautiful?"

"K-PAX sounds pretty damn good."

"Nothing good about the Earth? How about the mountains? The seashore? Music? You like opera?"

"Can't stand it."

"Why?"

"They're all just fucking glorified soaps. Make me want to puke," she added before waddling off and nearly running into Alice, who was in her "giant" phase, clomping through the lounge with enormous, loud steps. She shrugged Frankie off as if she were a mosquito.

It was times like these that I wished I had gone into some other line of work. Frankie always left me depressed. She holds all of us responsible for the death of her mother, who was given the wrong medication when she was in a hospital for some minor ailment. It was a famous case back then, and I remember reading about it myself. But accidents happen, even to the best of us, and Frankie might have come to realize that, had her father not killed himself a year later, followed by an older sister. (Ironically, the nurse responsible for the mix-up married Frankie's lawyer and became a wealthy and well-respected woman.) Though Frankie herself shows no tendency toward suicide, she remains hopelessly embittered toward everyone and everything. Of all the patients here she seemed the least likely to get any help from prot—he had a difficult time with human relations himself.

I heard a commotion behind me. "Dr. Brewer! Dr. Brewer!" Wondering what crisis was breaking this time, I turned to find Milton running toward me. "Uncle Miltie" wasn't wearing his usual funny hat, nor was his shirttail sticking out through his fly. In fact he looked like a different person altogether. It suddenly occurred to me that maybe this was the "real" Milton.

"Dr. Brewer!" he panted as he slid to a stop in front of me. "Let me out! Prot says I'm cured!"

"Well, Milton, I'd prefer you let the rest of us be the judge of that."

"No—you don't understand. I *am* cured."

"I know you believe that, and maybe it's true. Would you like to schedule an appointment so we can talk about it?"

"No need!"

"Really? Convince me. What makes you think you're well enough to leave us?"

"Prot says so."

I studied him for a minute. Gone were any obvious signs of psychosis. He was steady, clear-eyed, not going for laughs. This was a man who had lost his entire family in the holocaust. Not through some stupid mistake, as in Frankie's case, but as a result of one of the blackest periods in human history. Yet all the profound sadness underlying his jokes and clowning was no longer clouding his eyes. "Tell me—what happened to you today?"

"I spoke with prot. He had the answer to all my problems."

"What is that?"

"Forget our history."

"Forget the holocaust??"

"Forget everything! We don't have to live in the past, regretting everything we've done or that anyone else has done. We don't have to look for retribution, to continue the cycle over and over. We don't even have to forgive anyone. We can start all over, as if the events of the past never happened. This can be day one! It is for me!"

"Does this make sense to you, Milton?"

"Perfect sense, Dr. Brewer."

"And you think your memories won't come back?"

"Of course they won't. There *is* no past! This is the beginning of time!"

"I'd like to talk to you about this some more, but I want to speak with prot first. That okay with you?"

"Whatever you say. Should I plan to move down to Ward One?"

"That's up to Dr. Goldfarb and the assignment committee, but I think there's a good chance of that if you continue to improve."

"I guarantee it. You'd be surprised what a burden the past can be!"

"*That* I won't argue with!"

When I got back to my office our esteemed director was there, pacing back and forth, smoking a cigarette. Goldfarb stopped smoking ten years ago.

"What's wrong?" I asked her.

"You remember the visit we had from the CIA after prot's TV appearance two years ago?"

"How could I forget? They reminded me of Laurel and Hardy."

"Well, they're back."

"What did they want?"

"They wanted to know why we hadn't told them prot had returned. They wanted to talk to him."

"What did you tell them?"

"I asked them if they had a search warrant." Like my daughter Abby, Goldfarb is among the last of the liberals.

"Did they have one?"

"No. But they did have a request signed by the President."

"You mean *the* President?"

"The."

"How did they know prot was here?"

"Everyone seems to know that."

"So did you give them the go-ahead?"

"No. I said I had to speak to his doctor first."

"What do they want to talk to him about?"

"They want to know how he's able to travel at light speed. For security reasons, they tell me."

"I'm tempted to deny their request."

"Are you prepared to deny one from the President of the United States?"

"Maybe."

"Good! To tell you the truth, I didn't think you had it in you."

"But I think the decision should be up to prot."

She tamped out the cigarette on her watch crystal (an old habit) and dropped the butt into a jacket pocket. "That's only the beginning."

"What do you mean?"

"They want to be here when he leaves."

"What for?"

"Same thing. They want to set up cameras and all sorts of other equipment to record the event."

"How they going to get all that into his little room?"

"They've already thought of that. They want him to use the lounge."

"Of course you said no to that."

She examined her shoetops, which were suede and matched her green wool skirt. "Not exactly."

"What do you mean?"

"I offered them a compromise. I said only if we let the press in to cover it, too."

"What? You want to—"

"There's a difference between meddling in a patient's affairs and simply observing him. If they keep out of the way and don't try to interfere with whatever happens . . ."

"That's a pretty fine distinction."

"Look. The new wing is running a million and a half over estimates. We're going to need all the publicity we can get to generate the funds necessary to complete the goddamn thing."

I started to laugh.

"Something's funny?"

"I was just thinking: prot's going to love ending his visit with another fundraising appearance."

After she left I realized I had forgotten to tell her about Milton.

Session Thirty-seven

WHEN I entered prot's room on Wednesday morning, escorted by a couple of felines, he exclaimed: "Look what the cats drug in!" Several other inmates were in attendance.

I wasn't amused. "Prot, I need to talk to you."

"Anything you say, doc." A tiny nod and all the other patients trailed out, but not without a little muttering and nasty stares, even from the cats.

I sat down in his chair. "What did you tell Milton?"

"You mean about treating his life as a bad joke?"

"Yes."

"I told him to forget your history. It's nothing but a bloody mess, a catalog of false starts and wrong turns, doomed from the beginning."

"He should forget *all* of our history?"

"*Every* human being should forget it."

I wondered whether he was joking again. "Look, prot. I

appreciate your attempts to help the patients. We all do. But I don't think you should try to treat them without discussing it with their doctors first."

"Why?"

"Because mental illness is a very complex matter—"

"Not really."

"Prot, I know you've helped others in the past. But a wild suggestion like that could backfire if—"

"It worked, didn't it?"

"And in the second place, how can we forget our history? Someone has said that if we forget history, we are doomed to repeat it."

"You repeat it anyway! You have a war, then another war, then another and another. You never learn a thing from them, except how to kill more beings more efficiently. Your history serves mainly to remind you who to hate. But your petty wars and other peccadilloes are a small matter compared to your determination to destroy your own WORLD. Basically you got off on the wrong feet in the beginning. Everything you've tried—feudalism, communism, capitalism, nationalism, sexism, racism, speciesism—has failed. The only way to get out of a vortex like that is to start all over again."

I reminded myself never to argue with a crazy person. "Thanks. I'll pass that on. The other thing I wanted to talk to you about involves a couple of visitors we had yesterday."

"You mean the g-men."

"You know about them?"

"Everybody knows about them."

"So you know they want to speak to you."

"They want me to go to germany, too?"

"No, I think the TV demonstration convinced them you

can travel on a beam of light. But they want to know exactly how you do it."

"It's done with—"

"Mirrors. Yes, I know. Would it be all right with you if Giselle schedules a meeting between you and them?"

"If she wants."

I stood up. "When will she be coming in?"

"Any time now."

"She tells me she's going to K-PAX with you. Is that true?"

"If rob goes, she wants to go, too."

"And if he doesn't want to go? Or you can't find him?"

"I imagine she'll want to stay here with him. Odd, isn't it?"

"What's odd about it?"

"Your beings would rather live on a doomed PLANET than go to paradise and leave someone you love behind. It's a most interesting phenomenon."

"In any case, do you think you should get her hopes up like that?"

"I merely answered her questions. The hope is her own idea."

"But you *might* include her on your list."

"Many of the sapiens I've talked to would go if they had the chance. And almost *all* the other beings. You've made life on EARTH miserable for them, you know. It's turning out to be more difficult than I thought to narrow the list down to a hundred."

"Before you make a final decision, the residents of Ward Three want to speak with you as well. Will you come for lunch today?"

"Will there be fruit?"

"I guess that can be arranged."

"I'll be there!"

I needed coffee. In the doctors' dining room I found Laura Chang reading a journal and sipping a cup of tea. She had been with us only a couple of months and, as yet, I didn't know her very well, except that she came with a fine academic record and excellent recommendations. About all I knew for sure was that she had been a championship ice skater in her youth but had sustained an unfortunate injury that shortened her career and precluded a trip to the 1988 winter Olympics. As a result of this and the subsequent depression she became interested in medicine and then psychiatry.

I asked her how she was getting along with her patients, whether she had any unanswered questions about the hospital, or any problems with the staff or facilities.

"That pounding and drilling in the new wing is driving me crazy!" she replied without looking up from her article (on the relationship between autism and oxygen deprivation in the fetus).

"Well, it'll all be finished in another twenty or thirty years."

Chang was not amused. "It's like going to the dentist every day!"

I went for a cup of "rainforest blend." On the other side of the room I could hear Thorstein and Menninger discussing Cassandra. Or Thorstein, anyway. He has the kind of voice that would carry across Grand Central Station. It appeared that Cassie had withdrawn even more into her thoughts and dreams than ever. This was not unusual—all the patients have their ups and downs. What was puzzling, however, was that she seemed to be the one resident on whom prot was having a negative effect. Even prot can't win them all, I mused.

When I got back to Chang's table she was still buried in the journal. I gazed at her shiny black hair, the bright, youthful face, and for a moment I caught a glimpse of the future. Despite the astronomical expense of medical and psychiatric training, the cost-cutting outlook of the health-care providers, and all the other difficulties associated with the practice, I realized with no small degree of pleasure that the current crop of clinicians was among the best ever to come out of the various residencies. Maybe because the greater challenges aren't for the faint-hearted.

"Any other complaints?" I asked her. "Anything you want to talk about?" What I really wanted to know, of course, was whether she was having trouble with any of her patients.

She looked up from her article. "I *would* like to know more about prot."

"You mean about Robert. Prot is really only a secondary personality."

"But if I understood you correctly at the last staff meeting, you're having a problem getting through to Robert. What have you tried?"

Good God, I thought. She wants to help *me*. I didn't know whether to be flattered or insulted. But what the hell—maybe she could spot something I'd missed. I gave her a short summary of prot's first and second "visits," and a brief review of what had been accomplished, if anything, during our four sessions since his reappearance two weeks earlier.

"The whistle didn't bring him out this time?"

"Not as far as I could tell. He's withdrawn even deeper into his shell than he was when I first saw him seven years ago."

"But it worked before?"

"Yes."

"With hypnosis or without?"

"Without. It was a post-hypnotic suggestion."

"Ever try it when the patient was under hypnosis?"

My chin dropped. Then I burned the roof of my mouth. What a fool I was! It had been so easy to bring Rob forward in 1995 that I assumed hypnosis wouldn't be necessary this time around.

Without another word she returned to her journal. But her eyes were even brighter than before, and I'm almost sure there was a hint of a smile on her face.

The Thursday lecture was another disaster. When I reported that prot wouldn't cooperate in the light-travel experiment, there was a collective roar. A discussion broke out (as if I weren't even there) about whether this proved prot was only human after all. When I finally gained control and began to talk about eating disorders, there was a constant shifting in seats, shuffling of papers, coughing and hacking, and the inevitable, "Are we going to be responsible for this on the final exam?"

I was tired and went through the material as fast as possible. And, as before, I was preoccupied by thoughts of prot and all the unwanted complications his presence at the hospital always brought, though I had been informed that his joining the residents of Three for lunch the day before had had a considerable salutary effect. And there was definitely a change in Milton. Not only was he no longer telling endless jokes and juggling vegetables and riding around the lounge on his unicycle, he couldn't seem to do those things anymore, couldn't even *remember* any jokes. In the not inexpert opinion of Betty McAllister and some of the other nurses, he was as sane as they were, and should be transferred to Ward One, if not discharged immediately.

But what about Cassandra? Why had she become more withdrawn than she was on her arrival, and what did this have to do with prot? Of course my thoughts were focused primarily on Robert. I *had* to find him again, perhaps while his "alien" friend was under hypnosis. Failing that, I planned to go at him with what might have happened to him as a baby, jolt him into consciousness one way or another. I only hoped the shock wouldn't be just another short circuit.

Once again I withheld the bowl of fruit. I wanted prot to feel edgy, uncertain. He came into my examining room, glanced around, shrugged, and took his seat. "How are you today?" I asked him perfunctorily.

"Peachy keen," he replied, rather pointedly I thought.

"Have you seen the CIA yet?"

"Sí, señor, I see the cia by the seaside."

"What did you tell them?"

"I told them it was done with mirrors."

"What else?"

"They wanted to know if I'd explained the procedure to any foreign powers."

"Well?"

"I said, 'What you mean, "foreign," white man'?"

I concealed a weak grin. "And?"

"They wanted me to sign something promising I wouldn't do that."

"Did you?"

"No."

"What'd they say?"

"They offered me some stocks and bonds."

I couldn't hold back a snort. "Anything else?"

"They asked me not to try to leave this place."

"Did you agree to that?"

"I said I would stay until December the thirty-first. Except for a few brief excursions, perhaps."

"What did they think of your making 'excursions'?"

"They said they would be watching me."

"Since you brought that up, I wonder if you would tell me something I've been wondering about: How do you get out of the hospital without anyone seeing you?"

"Can you see a photon?" he asked with an all-too-familiar grin.

"But that's what light is composed of, isn't it?"

"More or less."

"Well, can you go through doors?"

"Now, gene, you know light doesn't go through doors."

"Does that mean if we put you in a room without windows you wouldn't be able to get out?"

"Of course not. I'd just open the door and leave."

"What if the door were locked?"

He wagged his head. To him I must have appeared to be the stupidest person on Earth. "Gino, there isn't a lock on

EARTH I couldn't open. But if you want to play another of your little games . . ."

"What if there were no door?"

"If there's no door, how would you get me in there?"

"Well, we could build the room around you."

"And what would keep me from leaving while the walls are going up?"

"Well, we could—" But time was passing rapidly, and there wasn't anymore to waste. "Ah, skip it. See that little dot on the wall behind me?"

He warbled, "That ooooooold black magic has me [pause] innnnnn its spellllll. . . . Onetwothreefour—" and dropped into his customarily deep hypnotic state.

I waited a moment before saying gently, though confidently, "Rob, would you please step forward for a moment? I have something very important to discuss with you."

There was no indication he had heard me.

"Rob, I think I might know what's bothering you. What's causing you so much anguish. May I tell you about it?"

I waited for another long minute. It was like speaking to the dead. Well, I thought, what can we lose? I pulled out the whistle and blew it as loudly as I could.

There wasn't a twitch, not a flutter. But of course he might have been faking a response in 1995. As a former mentor was fond of saying, "When all else fails, try a sledgehammer."

"Rob, I think you may have been abused in some way very early in your life, maybe when you were a baby. Something that you yourself may not even be aware of, and it ties in with your later encounters with Uncle Dave and Aunt Catherine. It was something terrible and it irreversibly changed your life, but whatever happened wasn't your fault, and we can repair the damage if you'll let us. Do you understand?"

No response.

"Rob? Can we talk about this for a minute?" I waited. "All right. If you'll just indicate in some way that you hear me, you can go for now. I won't bring this up again until you're ready to talk about it—okay?"

Not a nod, not a whisper.

"All right, Rob. Please think it over until we meet again in a few days. I'll see you then."

I waited for another little while. "Prot? Are you there?"

His eyes popped open. "Hiya, doc, how you been?"

"Peachy keen," I replied glumly. "I'm going to wake you up now. Five, four, three—"

"Are we done?"

"Apparently we're back to square one. Again."

"The best place to be!"

"In that case, let's start where we left off last time. You were six, in Earth terms, and so far you've had a perfect childhood on K-PAX, with no problems whatever, except for the odd scrape or bruise, of course." Missing or ignoring the hint of sarcasm, he waited for me to proceed. "What happened after that?" I prodded him.

"After what?"

"After you were six."

"I was seven."

"Har har har. Tell me about your life as a boy of seven. For example, did you have any friends your own age?"

"Everyone on K-PAX—"

"Let me rephrase that. Did you have anyone your age

to play—I mean, to interact with? Of your own species, that is."

"Not really. As you know, there aren't many children around. Not like on EARTH, where almost everyone seems to think it's his and her duty to breed and breed and choke your WORLD to death as quickly as possible."

I jotted down: Environment rantings really about procreation/sex? "Let's talk about *you* today, shall we? I remind you that if your parents hadn't conceived you, you wouldn't be here."

"If Giselle had wheels, she'd be a wagon."

"Do you think you shouldn't have been born?"

"Irrelevant, incompetent, and immaterial. I didn't get a vote in the matter."

"If you had gotten a vote, how would you have voted?"

"If Giselle had wheels, she'd be—"

"All right. Who did you associate with when you were a boy?"

"Whoever happened—"

"—to be around. Yes, of course. But could you be more specific?"

He named a few names, none of which I had heard before.

"Okay," I interrupted. "What sorts of things did you do with these—uh—beings?"

"The same as anyone does. We ate and slept and watched the stars and talked about all sorts of things."

"What sorts of things did you talk about?"

"Whatever came to mind."

At that point something came to mine. "Tell me: Who told you about the Earth?"

"No one told me. I heard your radio waves when I was in the library. Along with those of other PLANETS."

"How old were you then?"

"Oh, thirty-five or so. Three and a half in your terms."

"Are all K-PAXian kids interested in astronomy?"

"Oh, sure. K-PAXians love to talk about other PLAN-ETS, other GALAXIES, other UNIVERSES, that sort of thing."

"When did you first come to Earth?"

"You remember. In 1963, your calendar."

"How old were you then?"

"Sixty-eight."

"Was it your first trip to another planet?"

"No. But it was my first solo flight."

"I see. Do you remember the details?"

"Every one of them."

"Would you mind filling me in on them, please?"

"Not at all." But he just sat there.

I rephrased the question.

"I got a call from someone named 'robin.' He said he needed me. So I hopped on over."

"He called you on the telephone?"

"Of course not—we don't have telephones on K-PAX."

"So how did you know he needed you?"

"I suppose I happened to be tuned to his wavelength."

"His wavelength?"

"Have you forgotten *all* your high-school physics, gino? A wavelength is the length of a wave."

"And you just went."

"Yep."

"What were you doing when the call came?"

"Eating some likas. Watching a yellow hom dig a hole."

"And where did you land when you got here?"

"In china."

"How did you get to Montana?"

"Same way I got to china."

"Light travel."

"Kee-reck."

"So you found Rob—"

"In no time at all."

"What was he doing when you got there?"

"Attending a funeral."

"What did he say when you showed up?"

"Not much. His father had just died."

"So he was pretty unhappy?"

Prot paused here. "It was the first time I had encountered sadness. It took me a little while to understand what was wrong with him."

"What did you decide it was?"

"I figured it probably had something to do with his father's demise."

"Wouldn't that make you sad?"

"I don't know who my father is."

"Of course. So you couldn't possibly be sad when he dies."

"I probably wouldn't even know about it."

"How convenient."

"Is that another of your famous non sequiturs?"

"What did Robert want from you?"

"He didn't say. I think he just wanted someone to commiserate with."

"I can understand that. But why you?"

"You'll have to ask *him*."

"He doesn't seem to want to talk to me. Will *you* ask him?"

"Sure. If I see him."

"Thank you. Now—how long were you on Earth?"

"A few days."

"Just long enough to help him over the worst of it, is that right?"

"I suppose you could put it that way. After a while, he didn't need me anymore."

"So you went back to K-PAX."

"Righto."

"Back to your wanderings and stargazing and all the rest."

"Yes, indeedy."

"And that's how you spent your childhood."

"Pretty much. An orange or a banana would taste good right now, don't you think?"

"I'll see that you get some at the end of the session."

"Thankee kindly."

"No problemo. Now—how old were you when you got to puberty?"

"A hundred and twenty-eight."

"What's that like on K-PAX?"

"About like it is here. Hair sprouts up everywhere. Stuff like that."

"Any change in your feeling about girls?"

"Why should there be?"

"When did you become interested in girls?"

"I'm interested in everything."

"I mean sexually interested."

"You're playing dumb again, aren't you, gene? No one on K-PAX is sexually interested in anyone else."

"Because the sex act is so unpleasant."

"Very."

"Tell me—if it's so unpleasant, why do any of your beings want to produce children at all?"

"Not many of them do."

"Just enough to keep your species alive?"

"'Species' don't live. Only individuals do."

"I'll rephrase that. Your species propagates only enough to maintain itself?"

"No. As a matter of fact, our species will probably disappear in a few thousand years."

"Doesn't that bother you?"

"Why should it?"

"Why *should* it? Because there wouldn't be any more dremers (K-PAXians of prot's species)!"

He shrugged. "Here today, gone mañana. A drop in the ocean of time."

"All right. Tell me this: Is sexual activity unpleasant right from the start?"

"From the very beginning."

"Did you ever get an erection when you were a boy?"

"Once in a while."

"What was it like?"

"It usually meant I had to urinate."

"You never touched your penis except to urinate?"

"No."

"Did you ever have any sexual feelings when you had an erection, good or bad?"

"Pretty bad. I got up and peed right away."

"So, in your entire—ah—four hundred years or so, you've *never* been with a woman? Or a man, for that matter? Or masturbated, not even once?"

"Nothing could be farther from my mind."

"And no one ever made an attempt to seduce you at any time in your life?"

"Never."

"Have you ever seen anyone else do it? Of your own species, I mean."

"Do what?"

"Engage in sexual activity of any kind."

"No. It hardly ever happens on K-PAX, you know."

"You've never seen anyone kiss or touch someone of the opposite sex?"

"Of course we touch. But only in what you would call a 'platonic' way."

Something, no doubt extraneous, occurred to me. "If I remember correctly, you told me once that there is no such thing as marriage on K-PAX—is that right?"

"Yes, and may I say it's a pretty stupid idea on EARTH, too."

"Well, without love or marriage, how do you know who to produce a child *with*?"

"It's no big mystery. You bump into someone who, for some reason or other, feels a compulsion to add to the population of the species and—"

"How would you know if someone wants to do that?"

"He or she will tell you, of course. We don't have all these silly games you play on EARTH."

"Where do you 'bump into' members of the opposite sex? Are there bars? Things like that?"

"No bars. No restaurants. No exercise parlors. No grocery stores. No churches. No—"

"While you're traveling, then?"

"Usually. Or in the libraries. You'd be surprised how many interesting beings you can find in a library."

"And you just *do* it, without thinking much about it?"

"Oh we think about it very carefully before going ahead with it."

"You have to weigh the pros and cons."

"Exactly."

"And everyone on K-PAX knows how unpleasant sex is."

"Certainly."

"Who teaches you about that?"

"Whoever is—"

"Whoever is around. I know, I know. All right. What if someone wants to conceive a child with you and you don't want to do it?"

"Nothing."

"What about animals?"

Another little prot-like snicker. "We're all animals, gino."

"Did you ever see any other species on your planet copulate?"

"Once in a while."

"Do they seem to be in pain?"

"Absolutely. There's considerable resistance, a lot of noise and commotion."

"Do all your beings have this problem?"

"I don't consider it a problem."

"Prot, which do you hate most—money or sex?"

He wagged his head again. "You still don't get it, do you, doc? Money is a dumb idea. Sex is horrible."

I nodded, surprised to discover that our time was up.

But prot wasn't finished. "Your beings seem to be endlessly

fascinated by the subject of reproduction. That's all your popular songs are about, and your movies and sitcoms, etc., etc., ad nauseum. Love, sex, love, sex, love, sex. You humans aren't easily bored, are you?"

"It's an important subject for most of us."

"Pity. Think what you could accomplish if you spent all that time and energy on something else."

"We'll take this up next session, all right?"

"Whatever you say. Don't forget to have some fruit sent over. I'll be in my room."

"Just curious—what are you going to do after you've had the fruit?"

"Thought I'd take a nap."

"Sounds exciting."

"It can be." He flipped on his dark glasses. "Cheers."

I wondered what he meant by that. As he was going out the door, I shouted, "Prot!"

He whirled and peered over the dark glasses. "Yeeeesssss?"

"Do you ever dream when you sleep?"

"Sure."

"Try to remember one for next time, will you?"

"That won't be too hard. They're always the same."

"Really? What are they about?"

He rolled his eyes. "*Ka raba du rasht pan domit, sord karum—*"

"In English, please."

"Okay. I see a field of grains, with trees and beautiful flowers mixed in here and there. Nearby a couple of aps are chasing each other, and in the distance a bunch of—well, something like your giraffes are munching rummud leaves. A whole flock of mountain korms are flying by, barking their exuberant calls. . . ." He opened his eyes and gazed at the ceiling. "And the sky! The sky is like one of your sunsets—pink and purple all the time. You might say it's a picture-postcard scene, except we don't have pictures. Or postcards. The air is so clear you can see some of the rills on our closest moons. But the best parts of it you don't see. You feel and smell and taste them. It's so utterly calm that you can hear for miles. The air is sweeter than honeysuckle, only not as cloying. The ground is soft and warm. You can lie down anywhere. There is food wherever you look. And you are free to go anywhere without the slightest fear. Each moment is limited only by your imagination. And it's wonderfully peaceful. There's no pressure to work or do anything you don't want to do. Every single moment is a happy time, a time without—"

"All right, prot. It sounds great. I'll send you down a basket of fruit right away. What would you like?"

"Bananas!" he replied instantly. "I haven't had any of those for a while. The riper the better!" he reminded me.

"I remember."

He smiled in anticipation as he made his way to the stairs.

After he had gone I found myself scribbling: LOVE! SEX! LOVE! SEX! on my yellow pad. In fact I made it into a little tune. I had a feeling this had been a key session, yet I couldn't put my finger on exactly why. Was his problem a question of doing something almost unspeakable (in his mind) to someone he loved? Did this involve sex in some way? To prot, sex was the worst idea in the universe, worse even than his other bugaboos—money, religion, governments, schools, and all the rest. Despite his milk and honey protests, life was so calamitous for prot and his fellow "K-PAXians" that most of them would rather become extinct than reproduce themselves. I couldn't help feeling more than a little saddened by this terrible truth: The ultimate solution to his, and perhaps everyone's, problems was death itself. I didn't much like the ring of that.

Then there was the matter of dreams, a direct pipeline to the unconscious mind. There are whole journals devoted to the dream state, as well as to the phenomenon of sleep itself, though no one seems to know what purpose either of them really fulfills. It has been hypothesized (by Sagan, among others) that sleep evolved as a way to keep prey animals out of the clutches of predators during periods of highest risk. My own view is more or less the opposite: that sleep became a way to reduce anxiety and boredom while animals were in hiding. If so, it may serve the same function in human beings. In any case, the need for sleep has been with us for millions of years, as has, perhaps, the dream state.

The analysis of dreams can be a powerful component of psychotherapy. Dreams may be a way of bringing into the conscious mind events that are normally repressed. For example, a man who fears heights might persistently dream of falling out of windows. And a woman who is concerned about the sexual advances of a co-worker might dream of being attacked by men with clubs (phallic symbols). Though subject to more than one possible interpretation, dreams can give us important insights into what is literally "on someone's mind." Sometimes they can tell us things that don't come out even under hypnosis! Though it didn't seem likely that an analysis of prot's relentlessly idyllic one would be productive, I kicked myself for not making an effort to analyze Robert's dreams when I had had the opportunity. Now there were no dreams of Robert's to analyze. There was no Robert!

I kicked myself again.

SESSION THIRTY-EIGHT

O N SATURDAY, while raking the final leaves of autumn, I thought about a persistent dream of my own, one so familiar that I recognize it as a dream even as it happens. It always takes place in the same surroundings, my own house, though all the rooms are empty. After searching for a very long time (I don't know what I'm searching for), I step into a room and find a man there. He is carving something with a knife. I creep closer, trying to determine what he is whittling out. Closer and closer, until I can almost see the familiar figure in his strong hands. At this point I always wake up. Whether it's because I recognize it as the end of the dream or I don't really want to find out what he's carving, I can't say.

Of course it's my father, and it's my life he's forging for me.

I have other, more pleasant dreams as well: winning the Nobel prize for medicine (in my acceptance speech I can't think of a thing to say); passionate love with my wife, which sometimes turns into the real thing; playing basketball with my children, none of whom has ever grown up.

But prot had only one beautiful dream, as befit his singularly happy life in his perfect world. Where no one had to work, food was plentiful, and life was always fun, harmonious, and interesting. Had he always had this idyllic dream, even from the beginning? While stuffing the crunchy, redolent leaves into a large plastic bag, I thought about his previous "trip" to Earth and my serendipitous discovery of Robert, without which we might never have learned anything about his actual background. Suddenly I recalled asking prot, the first time he was under hypnosis, to relate the earliest experience he could remember. He replied, without hesitation, that it was Robert's father's funeral. Now he was claiming that he could remember being born, and even before. Could this be the wedge, the key, the inconsistency in his story I had been searching for?

Karen shouted that lunch was ready. The previous evening had been her retirement dinner, and nearly everyone there got up to tell a story about her career as a psychiatric nurse in one of Connecticut's finest general hospitals. For example, a colleague reminded us of the time she had missed lunch, and he had found her eating the leftovers of some of the patients, who later complained that they hadn't finished yet.

There were gifts, too, including *What's Your Opera IQ?*, a quiz book covering everything she might possibly want to know about the subject. Of course it was a joke. Karen hates opera, and accompanies me only so I'll watch her favorite old movies with her once in a while on TV. Nevertheless, I somberly thanked everyone for the thought, and promised to test her knowledge periodically. Other, more serious, gifts included travel and cookbooks, which she browsed through in bed half the night, the new bowling ball I had given her lying between us.

Though technically she had to go back before the end of the year to pick up her last check and take care of some loose ends, this was her first day of de facto retirement, and she had spent most of the morning in the kitchen simmering a hearty soup, kneading a sourdough bread, preparing a beautiful salad, and baking an apple pie for dessert. A far cry from my usual cottage cheese and crackers.

The rest of the afternoon was spent drowsily discussing family matters, making travel plans. One question that had put a damper (in my mind) on a permanent move to the country was what to do with the house I had grown up in with Karen right next door. In my mind's eye I watched her come out to play, her teeth sparkling, her nose freckled, her hair shining in the sun. I reminded her that I didn't want to lose all those wonderful memories.

"Don't be silly," she replied. "We'll rent it to one of the kids. Why don't you speak to Fred about it?"

I mumbled something and began to doze off.

"You'd better hang up your yellow pad pretty soon," she pointed out, "before you start falling asleep at meetings!"

I didn't tell her that had already happened more than once. But at least I hadn't yet fallen asleep with a patient.

The Monday staff meeting, usually a pretty somnolent affair itself, was rather animated this time. There was a great deal of excitement about the abrupt change in Milton, who had been with us for years and, we'd all assumed, would be here forever. Now he was waiting in Ward One for word that he would be discharged, and was eagerly anticipating life beyond these walls, regardless of what it held. It was the kind of thing we hope will happen to all our patients, but which rarely does.

This success, of course, brought more pressure for me to encourage prot to talk to all the other inmates, particularly those pathetic figures who seemed like permanent fixtures, among them Linus, Albert, Alice, and Ophelia. And, of course, Frankie. Everyone in the room seemed perfectly willing to give him the credit if these patients could be given a new lease on life, as had Milton and others before him, including even a couple of former psychopaths.

And I thought: Should I encourage prot to spend more time with these unfortunate beings? Did the potential good outweigh the risks to my own patient, Robert? It was the old ethics question come to life—was it right to sacrifice one person for the benefit of two or three others? I didn't know the answer then, and I don't know it now.

But one thing I did know: He wasn't going near any of the psychopaths this time, if I could help it. I didn't want someone like Charlotte, who had killed and disfigured at least seven young men, to take advantage of his openness and generosity. Even if he had no use for his genitalia, I didn't want him to lose them at the hands of a deranged psychotic.

"Onetwothree—" said prot before he fell into the familiar trance. I hadn't said a word.

"Can you hear me?"

"Of course."

"Good. Just relax. I'd like to speak to Robert for a moment." As long as prot was under hypnosis, there was nothing to lose by trying. Maybe Rob had thought about our last session, had a change of heart.

I waited for several minutes. He didn't come forward, of course, but I thought perhaps I could wear him down a little. "Rob? Did you think about what I said last time?"

No response.

"We're not going to discuss anything you don't want to talk about. I'd just like you to tell me whether you heard me at our last meeting, and whether you can hear me now. If you can hear me, please raise your left hand."

The hand didn't budge.

"Rob? We're wasting time. I know you can hear me. Now listen up. When you were here two years ago we talked about some of your problems, and we made great progress in solving them—remember?"

No response.

"When you were well enough to leave the hospital, you took a trip to your old home town, you started work on your bachelor's degree in field biology, you married Giselle and had a son. You named him Gene, after me. Okay so far?"

No response.

"I think you did that because you thought you owed me something. Well, I agree with you. You do owe me something. All I'm asking in return for everything we've accomplished together is for you to say you can hear me. That's all I'm asking. We can talk about whatever it is that's bothering you some other time. Fair enough?"

Nothing.

"Rob? I'm going to count to three. When I get to three, you're going to lift your left hand. Here we go: one . . . two . . . three!"

I looked hard at his hand, but not even a finger budged.

"All right, we're just going to sit here until you lift your hand."

We sat there, but the hand didn't move.

"I know you want to do it, Rob. But you're afraid of what will happen if you do. I assure you nothing will happen. This is your safe haven, remember? Nothing bad can happen to you here. Nor can you cause harm to anyone else. Do you understand? After you lift your hand you can go back and rest until next time. All right? Okay, here we go. Now—*lift your hand*!"

No response.

"Rob, I'm tired of screwing around. *LIFT YOUR GOD-DAMN HAND!*"

Not an iota.

"All right, Rob. I understand. You're feeling so bad that nothing matters to you. Not love, not loyalty, not your son, not anything. But consider this: I, Giselle, little Gene, your mother—did I tell you Giselle called her?—your classmates and friends, all the staff and residents at MPI, everyone you know wants to help you through this difficult period if you will only let us. Please think about that, will you? I hope you'll be feeling better the next time I see you. You may go now. Talk to you later," I added matter-of-factly. "Okay, prot. You can come back out."

He lifted his head and his eyes opened. "Hiya, doc. What's happening?"

"Not much, I'm afraid. But I hope that will change soon."

"For the better, I hope."

"So do I."

He closed his eyes. "Fivefourthree—"

"Wait!"

His eyes popped open again. "What? Am I doing it wrong?"

"No, not at all. But I'd like you to remain hypnotized for a while."

"What for?"

"Let's call it an experiment. How old are you now, by the way?"

"Three hundred—"

"In Earth terms, please."

"Thirty-nine years, ten months, seventeen days, eleven hours, thirty-two minutes, and—"

"That's close enough. Okay—now I want you to go back to when you were seventeen years old. In Earth terms, of course. You're rapidly getting younger. Robert is in high school. You visited him then. Do you remember?"

"Certainly. We talked about it earlier."

"Right. Rob's girlfriend Sarah had just become pregnant. He didn't know what to do."

The young prot shifted some imaginary gum in his mouth. "He was in deep shit, as you humans so elegantly put it."

"And you came to help him out."

He shook his head. "People—there seems to be no end to their problems!"

"All right. We've been over that before. Now I want you to go back to the time you were nine Earth years old, which is about ninety on K-PAX, right? You're becoming younger and younger. A hundred and twenty, a hundred, and now ninety. Understand?"

"Uh huh. I'm ninety."

"Right. You've just turned ninety. There aren't any birthday presents, of course. Does that bother you?"

"Why should it?"

"Okay. What are you doing right now?"

"I'm looking at the yort trees over by the adro field. I think I'll go and eat a couple of yorts."

"Okay. You do that. Who else is around?"

"Some ems are jumping about in the trees. I see a korm flying above them, and a lot of aps running around in the field. . . ." It was obviously a peaceful and beautiful prospect, like his only dream.

"Any other dremers around?"

"Only one."

"Who is he?"

Ninety-year-old prot chuckled. "He's not a he. He's a she."

"Your mother?"

"No."

"An aunt? A neighbor?"

"We don't have any of those on K-Pax."

"A stranger? Someone you don't know?"

"No."

"What's her name?"

"Gort."

"Is she a special friend of yours?"

"Every being is a friend."

"Nothing remarkable about Gort?"

"Every being is remarkable."

"Have you known her long?"

"No."

"All right, prot. You're getting younger now. Younger . . . Younger . . . We're going to go back to the time you were fifty years old."

Prot's eyes closed immediately. After that he didn't move. I waited. He still didn't move. I was beginning to worry that something might have happened to him. At the same time, I found myself unspeakably elated: Had this devastating period (age five) in Robert's life somehow affected the mind of fifty-year-old prot as well?

"Prot?"

No response.

I was definitely becoming concerned. "Prot? Listen carefully. We're going to go forward again to when you were ninety, okay? You're getting older now. You're sixty, seventy, eighty. Now you're ninety again. Please open your eyes."

They popped open. He seemed a bit confused.

"We were talking about Gort, remember?"

"Yes."

"Good. Bear in mind now that you are ninety years old. I want you to tell me something you *remember* about your eightieth birthday."

"We don't have birthdays on—"

"Yes, yes, I know. I mean, tell me what you were doing when you became eighty years old."

"I went to K-REM."

"What is that—another planet?"

"No. It's one of our purple moons."

"What's it like?"

"Like your sahara desert."

"How long did you stay?"

"Not long."

"Did you go with someone else?"

"Yes."

"A man?"

"Yes."

"How old is he?"

"Eight hundred and eighty-seven."

"Must have been one of his last trips."

He shrugged.

"All right. Now you're getting younger again. You're eighty and still getting younger. Seventy-five, seventy, sixty-five. Okay, now you're sixty. What are you doing at this moment?"

Prot's eyes closed again.

I waited, but he said nothing.

"Okay, prot," I said quickly. "You're getting older again. You're sixty-five, sixty-eight, sixty-nine, seventy. At this moment you're seventy again. What are you doing right now?"

"Seeing how far I can jump."

"Okay. Now listen carefully. I want you to tell me something that happened to you when you turned sixty years old."

He pondered the question for a moment. "I don't remember."

The hairs on the back of my neck began to tingle. "You don't remember when you were sixty?"

He fiddled with the arm of his chair. "No."

"Nothing at all?"

"No."

"What's the earliest thing you remember?"

With no hesitation he said, "I remember a casket. Before that it's a bit hazy."

I could actually feel the muscles in my chest tighten. "What can you tell me about that hazy period just before you saw the casket?"

The young prot frowned hard with concentration. "I'm

down on the ground," he murmured. "Someone is bending over me."

"Who is it? Who is bending over you?"

"I don't know her. She is wiping my face with something."

"She is cleaning you?"

"I suppose so. I'm groggy. And my head hurts."

"Why does your head hurt?"

"I don't know. I think I fell out of a tree. But I don't remember. . . ."

"Now this is important, prot. How old were you when this happened?"

"Sixty-eight."

"And you don't remember anything that happened before you were sixty-eight?"

He sniffed and wiped his nose on his shirt sleeve. "No."

My God! I thought. The seminal moment didn't come with Robert's abuse when he was a baby, or even at age five with Uncle Dave, but later! It was something that happened about the time of his father's death. Something so horrible that it overshadowed all the other terrible things that had befallen him. Did he actually witness his father's demise? Or even his suicide? Was it possible that he was asked to *assist* in it? Could it have been—God Almighty—a mercy killing? I saw that our time was almost up, and perhaps just as well. I needed to think about all this.

"Okay, prot, I'm going to bring you back to the present. You're beginning to get older. You're seventy-five now, and rapidly getting older. Eighty, ninety. Now you're a hundred, two hundred, three hundred, and now we're back to the present time, and you're here on Earth. Do you understand?"

"Of course I understand, doc. What's the big deal?"

"Good. Very good. Now I'm going to wake you up. I'm going to count backward from five to one, and—"

"I know all that. Fivefour—Hiya, coach. We done for the day?"

"Almost. I just want to ask you a couple more questions."

"Will they *never* end?"

"Not until we get some answers. Tell me what you remember about your sixty-eighth—I mean, tell me about the day you became sixty-eight years old."

"Haven't we—"

"Yes, but I want to hear it again."

He repeated, quickly and mechanically, "I got a call from someone named 'Robin.' He said he needed me. So I hopped on over. It was the first time I had encountered sadness. It took a little while to understand what was wrong with him. . . ."

"His father had just died."

"Yes."

"What do you remember before that?"

"Everything."

"Being born, and all that."

"Yep."

"Prot, are you aware that when you were under hypnosis you couldn't remember anything that happened to you before you were sixty-eight?"

"Get out of town!"

"How do you explain that?"

"Explain what?"

"That you can't remember any of that stuff when you're under hypnosis."

"No idea, coach. Unless it has something to do with the kroladon."

"The what? What's a kroladon?"

"A memory-restoring device."

"Your memory was restored with this thing?"

"Clever deduction, gino."

"Why didn't you tell me about this before?"

"It never came up."

The tape of this session is silent for a full two minutes. Finally I sighed and asked him, "How does this 'device' work?"

"Search me. I think the kroladon doesn't actually restore memory, but only re-imprints it on different circuits."

"All right. How did you lose your memory?"

"I'm a little unclear about that. You see, there's a little gap between the time you lose it and when the kroladon re-programs it. Otherwise—"

"Well then, damn it, *when* did you lose it?"

"When I was sixty-eight."

"Just before your first trip to Earth."

"Pre-SOISS-ly."

"At pre-SOISS-ly the time of Robin's father's death!"

Without looking at the clock, which showed that our session was over, prot suddenly exclaimed, "Fruit time!" and hurried out.

I didn't try to stop him.

This was crazy, an absurd situation. Contrary to all logic, the *unhypnotized* prot could remember, with the help of a "memory-restoring device," events in his life beginning with the womb, while the *hypnotized* prot couldn't remember a thing that happened before his "sixty-eighth" birthday.

Perhaps because he didn't exist prior to that time? Did he *create* his own early childhood? Was the "kroladon" *him*? I could hear my former mentor David Friedman cajoling me to "pursue, pursue, pursue." On the other hand, he was also fond of uttering gibberish like "How now brown cow?" at the most unexpected times. Helped him to think, I suppose.

I mumbled that phrase three or four times, but didn't come up with anything at all, except for an image of a puzzled cow. I did, however, decide to pursue, pursue, pursue, no matter where it led.

Giselle had come up with a list of Robert's likes and dislikes, and from that came a few suggestions for the things he probably missed most in his current noninteractive state. Things like his son, Giselle herself, his mother, mushroom and black olive pizza, and chocolate-covered cherries. And, of course, his father. Not much we could do about that, but maybe something could be done with the rest.

I remembered the hint of a reaction when I had mentioned his mother. "But that might have been wishful thinking," I confessed.

"Should we get her to pay him a visit?"

"I doubt it would help. She was here before when he was catatonic, remember? He never even acknowledged her presence, and all it did was upset her even more."

Her eyes lit up. "I bet he'd respond pretty fast if his father came to see him!"

"Giselle, you know that's impossible."

"Is it? I have an actor friend who could play him pretty

well if we get him something to base it on! Do you think it might be worth a try?"

I had to admit it might jolt something out of Rob. The other side of the coin, of course, was that it might make matters even worse. But time was running out and, at this point, maybe anything was worth trying.

"The only problem," she added, "is that he's rehearsing for Off-Broadway. But I'll see if he can squeeze it in."

"Okay, but let's not rush into anything. I've got something else in the fire." I told her about prot's inability to remember his early childhood under hypnosis, and my plans to pursue this.

Her only reaction was a stunned, "Is that possible?"

I shrugged. "Where prot is concerned, anything's possible!"

On my way through the Ward Two lounge the next morning I came across Alice and Albert chatting animatedly on the big green sofa. "Alex Trebek" was hanging around, apparently serving as moderator. I marveled, as always, at how far advanced a mental institution is compared to the outside world: a young black woman, an older Chinese–American, and a middle-aged Caucasian deep in conversation with no consideration of age, race, gender or nationality. Here, everyone is equal. Maybe prot was right—all our differences are based on past mistakes and cruelties, and if we could somehow forget our respective histories and start over, who knows what might come of it.

Of course they clammed up as I approached. But I soon learned that all three had been given certain "tasks" to perform. A familiar uneasiness set in.

"May I ask who gave you these 'tasks'?"

"Why, prot, of course," Alice proudly informed me.

"That's right!" Alex verified.

I had mixed feelings about this revelation, but I had learned not to rush to judgment in matters involving our alien visitor. "And what 'tasks' did prot assign to you, Alice?"

She deferred to Albert, who replied, "Theoretically, very simple ones. You see, Alice has a problem with space, and I with time. But prot pointed out that the space–time continuum is a kind of symbiosis, whereby space can be increased at the expense of time, and vice versa. If we can learn to trade one for the other, we would both be cured!"

I resisted the temptation to remind them that their doctors would be the judge of that. They all seemed so pleased that there might be a simple answer right around the corner that I didn't have the heart to discourage them.

"What about you, Alex? Did prot give you something to do, too?"

"Yes!"

Albert explained that prot had suggested he do his own show right here in the hospital.

"Will you be setting that up, Alex?"

"Correct!"

"He's going to get to work on it right after lunch," Alice added.

"How about you, Albert? You and Alice getting right to work, too?"

"Immediately. In fact, we were just discussing it when you came along." They all stared at me impatiently.

I took the hint. "Well, I've got to run. Good luck to all three of you!"

No one offered a farewell. They were already back to whatever they had been considering earlier. Their tasks seemed harmless enough, I thought, and might take their minds off their problems, if only for a little while.

On my way out to find prot, I literally bumped into him. Or would have, had he not stepped aside at the last moment, though he didn't seem to be looking in my direction. "It was the best I could do on short notice," he volunteered, when he finally noticed me.

"What—the 'tasks' you've been giving out?"

"Isn't that what you wanted to see me about?"

"Well, that was one thing. Actually, I have no problem with any of that as long as the patients' expectations aren't raised too high."

"All I can do is point the way. The rest is up to them."

"Well, we'll see how successful your 'treatment program' is. But the other reason I was looking for you was to invite you to the house for Thanksgiving tomorrow."

"What—and watch you cut open a dead bird? No, thanks."

"Well, how about the day after? What about Friday?"

"Relax, gino. Take a weekend off. Anyway, I won't be here Friday."

"What do you mean you 'won't be here'?"

"Is that a difficult concept for you?" He repeated each word slowly and distinctly. "I—won't—be—here." As if to emphasize his point, he turned to go.

"Where are you going? You're not leaving the hospital again, are you?" I called after him.

"Not for long!" he shouted back.

SESSION THIRTY-NINE

THIS YEAR Thanksgiving happened to fall on my birthday. Abby and her family came for the occasion, along with Will and his fiancée. They arrived early, Abby bearing the turkey (much to my surprise—she's a devout vegetarian), and Dawn helped with the preparations. I played a couple of games of chess with the boys (I could still beat them, though not by much), but it only reminded me of Ward Two and the slow-moving matches in the game room, which led to thoughts of prot and his "temporary leave" from the hospital.

I was still preoccupied with that dilemma when my son Fred, who had finished the tour with *Les Mis*, and daughter Jenny, all the way from California, made an unexpected appearance. It was the first time in years the whole family had been together.

Both of them hugged me, but all I could think to say was, "What are you two doing here?"

"It's Thanksgiving, Daddy, remember?"

"And Mom's retirement," Freddy added.

"And your birthday."

"It was supposed to be a surprise." They each handed me a package.

I wasn't surprised—I was dumbfounded. "I suppose your mother put you up to this."

"Well, she was in on it, but it was actually prot's idea," Fred replied.

"Prot?"

"He came to see us last month."

"Last month??"

At that point the kitchen contingent burst in, there was another round of hugs and kisses, and we were soon on our way to the dining room, happily accompanied by our other guest, Oxeye Daisy. I won't go into detail about the dinner, except to say that it was the most beautiful, and also the first, soy turkey I had ever eaten.

None of us has ever been much on public (or private) speaking, but I thought I should say something on the occasion of my sixtieth. So, after we were all completely stuffed, I rambled awhile about the delights and significance of having one's family around, how this becomes more and more meaningful with the passage of time, and so on. "For this I guess we have prot to thank," I added. "And I thank all of you wonderful people for being here."

Perhaps to shut me up, Freddy now raised his glass and said, "To prot!" and we all clinked ours against those within reach.

After the usual chitchat about the year's events, the strange weather, and the football standings (Abby's husband Steve toasted the Jets, who were still in the running), Will stood up. Across the table, Karen gave me a huge, knowing smile. We had both been waiting for them to select a wedding date. "Dawn and I are going to be parents!" he announced.

There were cries of joy and more clinking. Far too diplomatic to press them on when they were planning to tie the knot, "Grandma" asked our daughter-out-law when the baby was due.

"In June," Dawn replied cheerfully.

Jenny raised her glass. "To June!"

"To the new baby!" Abby chimed in.

"Happy birthday, Dad," Fred added.

"Have a great retirement, Mom," offered Will.

"To Oxie!" cried Star.

"*La chiam!*" Rain shouted. Clink. Clink. Clink.

I don't know why, but sad, happy tears began to roll down my cheeks. I took a sip of wine, hoping no one would notice.

Will disappeared and came back with a huge devil's food cake (my favorite) ablaze with what seemed like a dangerous number of candles. Having practiced for this moment, I proceeded to blow them all out, one at a time, around and around, except for the one in the center, which refused to be extinguished. There were groans all around.

"That one's prot's," thirteen-year-old Rain announced confidently. "Mom, can I have some wine?" Abby gave him a sip of hers. Nothing timid about that boy, I thought proudly. Maybe we have another doctor in the family!

Ever the optimist, Karen pointed out that sixty is the

beginning of the second half of your life, when you get a chance to do all the things you didn't get around to in the first half. "Unless you wait until it's too late," she added, holding my gaze meaningfully.

Later, after the presents had been opened (I got a "retirement planner" from Karen), I took Will aside and asked him how medical school was going.

"Great!" he told me.

"Still thinking about psychiatry?"

"No doubt about it."

We gabbed about what he was learning in med school and the rewards (and headaches) of residency and practice. I thought: Nothing can be better than this! I only wished my own father, the small-town doctor, could have been here with us.

"Your mother was wondering when you and Dawn are getting married."

"I don't know, Pop. Maybe never."

"Do you think that's the best thing?"

"It all seems so irrelevant."

"Maybe for you, but how about the baby?"

"Dad, you need to have a talk with prot."

The rest of the family drifted in. Freddy and I sang a few Broadway tunes. Fred is a far better singer than I ever was, but I like to think he got his talent from me. The grandchildren performed a little comedy skit. I don't know who they got that from.

I usually go in to my office on the Friday after Thanksgiving, but this time, despite the guilt feelings, I stayed home. Abby and her family, along with Will and Dawn, left on Thursday evening, but both Fred and Jenny stayed over. Freddy was going back to his own apartment in the city that afternoon because his beautiful ballerina-girlfriend was returning from a visit with her own family, and Jenny wasn't flying back to San Francisco until Sunday.

Although his mother resisted the temptation to suggest that Fred follow his younger brother's example, she nonetheless asked him some pointed questions about his "roommate," whom we had rarely seen. Poor Fred finally blurted out, "Laura doesn't want any children!"

After an embarrassing silence the conversation turned to Jenny's specialty, the treatment of patients suffering from AIDS. She was quite optimistic about the whole thing, reporting that deaths from the disease were on the decline for the first time in its history, and that a vaccine was on the way. When I made the facetious comment that she would soon have nothing to do, she reminded me that thousands of people were still dying from HIV infections every year, and the global incidence of the virus was still on the rise. I remembered an earlier comment by prot that some day human beings would be devastated by diseases "that would make aids look like a runny nose." I only hoped I wouldn't be around long enough to see that.

When I had a chance to talk to Freddy alone, I learned that after finishing his national tour he was, once again, "temporarily unemployed." This gave me an idea. I told him about the situation with Robert, that perhaps the only thing that might shake him out of his present state might be an appearance by his father.

He said, "Sure," and asked to see pictures of Mr. Porter,

and a description of what his voice might have sounded like. I told him I would send him a couple of photos from the file and have Giselle contact Rob's mother about her husband's manner of speaking and anything else that might be helpful.

After his reaction to the question about his apartment mate, I deferred inquiring about what he thought about taking over the house if we decided to vacate it. Instead, I asked my son, the former airline pilot, whether he ever missed flying.

"Do you miss getting your teeth drilled?" he replied.

At about lunchtime there was a call from Dr. Chakraborty. I took it in the den, where I still, even at this late date, felt I was imposing on my father's private sanctuary. "Hello, Chak. What's up?"

"There is bad news and there is also bad news," he informed me gravely.

I sighed, "Tell me the bad news first."

"You are not going to believe this," he assured me.

"Believe what?"

"It is the DNA work. There is no question about it. Prot and Robert Porter's DNAs are entirely different. It is confirmed."

"How different?"

"The odds they are not coming from the same person are seven billion."

"But—"

"I told you you would not be believing it."

I gazed at my desk, which was even more cluttered than the one in my office, and promised myself I would wade through it all sometime soon. "Chak, let's write a paper on this."

"It can be done. But no one will be believing it."

"You're probably right. Okay, what's the other bad news?"

"Prot has disappeared once more."

"Did anyone see him leave?"

"No. He was here one minute and gone away the next."

"Don't worry. He'll be back."

"I am not worrying."

I wasn't worried, either. He had done this before, and had always returned. But something else occurred to me on the way to the dining room: *Would Paul and Harry's DNA also be different from Robert's?* Indeed, might this be a simple way to diagnose multiple personality disorder? A Nobel prize, I dreamily reflected, would be as good a way as any to end a career. . . .

By the time of the Monday meeting the entire staff knew that prot had disappeared and there were the usual questions about how he had managed to slip through our fingers again. I reported that I had asked Betty McAllister to make sure someone kept an eye on him at all times, but he had managed to get the nurses to rescue a cat from a closet shelf and when they turned around he was gone. As before, the surveillance cameras in the corridors and at the gates recorded nothing of him at all, and a search of the premises also proved fruitless. Still, no one seemed overly concerned about his disappearance, and I thought: It's amazing how quickly we get used to even the most bizarre events.

On the other hand, no one was prepared for my summary of the previous session with him, in which the hypnotized prot couldn't remember anything of his early childhood, nor for the results of the DNA analysis. Both seemed preposterous, and there was no hesitation in telling me so. Before I could mention that I had already thought of it, Goldfarb recommended getting DNA samples from the other alters. Chang suggested I focus in on the precise moment that prot lost his memory and compare this to the exact time Robert called him to Earth. Menninger wondered whether the results of the last session might not mean that his so-called memory of K-PAX was contrived. Thorstein also "smelled a rat."

The meeting was interrupted by a tap on the door. Betty stepped in to let us know that prot was back and that someone had seen him at the Bronx zoo over the weekend. "My God!" Goldfarb exclaimed. "He's taking the animals!"

I wasn't going to provide any fruit for prot, but after he had somehow managed to bring the whole family together for Thanksgiving, I couldn't refuse him. There was also a mushroom and olive pizza, freshly baked in the hospital kitchens, and some chocolate-covered cherries from Lilac Chocolate in the Village, supplied by Giselle.

While he was scarfing down the various fruits as if there were no tomorrow, I turned on the tape recorder. "First of all, I want to thank you for getting Fred and Jenny to come for the holiday. How did you do that?"

"I just asked them."

"If *I* had asked them, they might not have showed up."

"That's one of the most interesting things about your species. Most humans will respond to an obviously unselfish request, even when they would refuse a selfish one. A remarkable trait, don't you think?"

"Secondly, you want to tell me where you've been the past few days?"

"Oh, out speaking with some of my friends."

"You mean non-human friends?"

"Mostly."

"In the zoo, for example?"

"Among other places."

"Are you taking some of them to K-PAX?"

"One or two, maybe."

"There's something I'm curious about."

"There's hope for you yet, doctor b."

"Won't that—bringing back alien species to K-PAX—screw up the ecology on your planet?"

"Not unless they develop human views on the subject."

"But—oh, never mind." I knew I wouldn't get anywhere with this.

Even though it was still three hours to lunchtime, the aroma coming from the covered tray was beginning to make my mouth water. "You want some pizza?" I asked him.

"Not if that's cheese I smell in there, and I think it is."

"Oh, for God's sake, prot, what's wrong with cheese? Nobody killed any cows to get that."

He snorted, a testament to my bottomless ignorance, I suppose. "Maybe you should look into that a little deeper."

"I'll do that," I promised him. "But first I'd like to speak with Robert."

"Onetwo—" His head fell to his chest so abruptly that

I wondered whether Robert might be eagerly waiting to come out.

"Rob?"

He wasn't.

"Rob, I've got some surprises for you. Smell that pizza?" I reached over and lifted out a slice. The cheese strung out more than a foot. "Here. Go ahead."

He didn't move a muscle. I took a noisy bite myself—anything for science. "It's delicious," I informed him. "Your favorite kind."

There was no response.

"Well, maybe you're right. A little early, isn't it? Okay. How about a chocolate-covered cherry? Just one won't hurt."

He wasn't the slightest bit interested. To encourage him, I tried a couple. They were wonderful.

I offered him an evening with Giselle, a visit from his son, even one from his mother. He didn't seem to care about any of this. I played my hole card. "Your father may be coming to see you soon. Would you like that?"

I thought I saw one of his hands twitch briefly and heard a muffled sound of some kind, but it didn't show up on the tape of this session. I waited for a moment in case he changed his mind about coming out. He didn't. "All right, prot. Come on back."

He quickly raised his head. "*Finito?*"

"For the moment. Please unhypnotize yourself."

"Fivefour— Find him yet?"

"No, I didn't. Any suggestions?"

"Perhaps you're barking up the wrong tree."

"What tree would you suggest I bark up?"

"I was thinking of the tree of knowledge."

I glared at him. "Last time you told me about a 'memory-restoring device,' remember?"

"Of course."

"There's something about the—uh—'kroladon' that I don't understand."

"I'm not surprised."

Prot seemed to be getting more arrogant every day. But perhaps that was just my own frustration coming out. Or maybe it was *his*. "Does it bring forth *all* your memories? Even the bad ones?"

"We don't have bad memories on K-PAX."

"I see. So if I asked you something about your past, anything at all, you'd tell me?"

"Why not?"

"Even if it were uncomfortable for you?"

"Why would it be uncomfortable?"

"All right. Let's talk some more about your childhood on K-PAX."

"You seem to be obsessed with childhood, gino. Is that because your own was so terrible?"

"Dammit, prot, when this is over, you can ask me any questions you like. Until then, we'll concentrate on *you*. Okay?"

"It's your party."

"Some party. Now—I want you to think back again to your boyhood on K-PAX. You're fifty-nine point nine now. Understand?"

"I think I can manage that."

"Good. Great. Okay, you're sixty now, and time is passing rapidly. You're watching the stars, eating, talking and running with your friends of whatever species, the days—I mean the time—is going by, and soon you're sixty-eight point one. Some more time goes by, and you become sixty-eight point two. And so on. Point three, point five, point seven, point nine. Do you remember anything about those days?"

"Everything."

"Naturally. Now I'd like to put you under again."

"Under what?"

"Prot, please just go to sleep."

"One—"

"Prot? Can you hear me?"

"Of course."

"Good. Now I want you to think back to the time you were sixty-eight point five. What do you remember about that time in your life?"

He thought for a moment. "Nothing."

"Can you describe something that happened when you turned sixty-eight point six?"

"I remember looking up at the stars."

"Is this the first thing you remember?"

"Yes."

I sat bolt upright. "Go on."

He put his hands against his temples and frowned. "My head hurts. I remember wandering toward K-MON for a while. I came to a balnok tree and smelled its bark. Balnok bark smells terrific! I chewed on some, then I found a rock that I hadn't seen before, and I asked someone what it was. He told me it was a silver ore, and the blue and green veins were morgo and lyal salts. It was so lovely that I—"

"Excuse me. Were you wearing any clothes at the time?"

"No. Why should I?"

"What about the man?"

"No. And he wasn't a man. He was a cras [pronounced 'crass']."

"What's a 'cras'?"

"A progenitor of the dremers."

"The dremers evolved from the crasses?"

"That's another way to put it."

"Did he harm you in any way?"

"Of course not."

"What happened after he told you what the rock was?"

"He went his way and I went mine. In a little while I got a call from—"

"All right. We'll return to this later. Right now I want you to go back just a bit. Something happened to you earlier. Maybe you fell out of a tree—something like that. You might have been knocked out. When you woke up, you had a headache and you were lying on the ground. Someone was wiping your face, and you couldn't recall what had happened to you. Do you remember that moment?"

He closed his eyes. "Uh—"

"Do you remember what happened to you? How you came to be lying on the ground with a headache?"

He frowned hard and then stared at the ceiling as if trying to find some answers there.

"Try to remember, prot. It's very important."

"Why?"

"Prot—please try to cooperate! I think we may be getting somewhere."

"Where?"

The tape indicates that I took a long, deep breath at this

point. "I don't know yet. For now, please try to remember how you got that headache!"

He paused again. "I—there's a—a dremer. He is lying in a hollow log. I am cleaning him with a fallid leaf. . . ."

"Tell me more about this—uh—being. What does he look like? Is he young or old?"

"Not old, but not young, either. He is broken. He is in—in great pain, and—I don't remember anything else."

"Try!"

"I remember running. I am running, running, running as fast as I can. I'm running so fast that I bang against a tree. Then someone is wiping my face. My head hurts. . . ."

"Okay, what happened after that?"

"I found some balnok bark to chew on, but the headache didn't go away. I told you about the silver ore. Later on, I heard someone calling me. It was Robert. He needed me, and I went to help him."

"Don't you think it a little strange that someone would call you for help right after you lost your memory?"

"Not really. Beings are crying out for help all over the UNIVERSE."

"I see. All right—this is your first experience with inter-planetary travel, right?"

"No. I'd been doing that for quite a while."

"You had traveled to other planets?"

"I'd been skipping around our solar system since I was twenty-five or so. As a passenger, of course."

"But none of these trips came about as a result of your being 'called for help' by someone."

"Nope."

"And—even though you had never even been out of your

own solar system—on your first trip to another one you travel halfway across the galaxy by yourself."

He shrugged. "That's where your PLANET *was*."

"Weren't you afraid? Didn't it bother you to be so far away from home at so young an age?"

"Home is wherever we are. The UNIVERSE is our home."

"Who told you that?"

"Everyone."

"No small-town family ties for K-PAXians, right? But didn't you feel the need to have an adult go with you? To get you out of trouble if need be?"

"Why should I get into trouble?"

"Well, you might run into some dangerous animals, for example."

"I did."

"You did?"

"Yes. Homo sapiens."

"All right. Let's go back to the time just before you got the call. You were bathing someone. Do you know who it was?"

"No."

"Concentrate, prot. You were bathing this man, and suddenly you started running. Why?"

"I— He—"

"Take your time."

"Something was wrong."

"What was wrong, prot? What was wrong?"

"I don't know. That's where it's fuzzy. The next thing I remember is running away from him." He was becoming agitated.

I hated to close this session, but, unfortunately, I had to attend a fundraising luncheon (one of the things I had tried unsuccessfully to eliminate from my cluttered schedule) on Long Island. I was tempted to skip it, but I was the featured speaker. "All right, prot, you may unhypnotize yourself."

"Five—"

"That's all for today. I'll see you on Friday."

He left, but without the usual jaunty step, or so it seemed to me. I, too, was washed out, and I finished off the pizza and chocolates. Perhaps, I thought, I can make the talk a short one.

To my surprise, the CIA was present at the fundraiser, along with several members of the press. Both groups stared at each other suspiciously. I have no idea how they got wind of the event, but the whole thing took on an entirely different character.

I began by describing progress on the new wing, and how it would provide needed space for new facilities and instrumentation to carry out important research well into the twenty-first century. Before I got any farther, however, someone asked a question about prot. I admitted he had returned, but declined to comment on the nature of his treatment. Nonetheless she (and others) persisted: Who was he, really? Where had he been? Could he really do all the things I had reported in my books, particularly travel faster than the speed of light? How long was he staying? Where was he going? Who was he taking with him? Was he really behind some of the "miraculous" cures we had achieved in recent years? Why were so many people hanging around in front of the hospital? And on and on. Unfortunately, I didn't have many of the answers. Indeed, it occurred to me that I really didn't know very much about prot, about multiple personality disorder, about anything.

And the lunch was no picnic, either. I toyed with a plate of linguine (with a sauce of wild mushrooms and black olives), and couldn't even look at the Death by Chocolate cake. My stomach was churning and the unanswerable questions kept coming. It was like a nightmare. Worst of all, there wasn't a single financial contribution, much to the chagrin of Virginia Goldfarb and our financial officer, who were becoming more and more frustrated by the cost overruns associated with the construction of the new wing, another affair I was nominally in charge of.

The next morning, just as the sun was coming up, it finally dawned on me why Cassandra might have been a little depressed recently—she may have seen something in the skies that indicated she wouldn't be among the passengers selected for the journey to K-PAX. But, if so, she might well have some information on who *would* be going, especially now that the time of departure was rapidly approaching. Of course I didn't expect a mass exit on New Year's Eve, a flock of patients streaming into the heavens like a gaggle of featherless geese. But if I could get the names of those on the "waiting list," it might help the staff deal with the terrible, though certain, letdowns among those who were lining up for the trip.

Prot, prot, prot. Where have you come from and where are you going? How is it that some people, or even their alter egos, are able to convince others they know all the answers, hold the keys to the kingdom? Can anyone explain how a charismatic figure can talk three dozen people into taking a cyanide trip to Comet Hale-Bopp? And these weren't even residents of a mental institution!

In the shower I didn't have enough energy to sing the toreador song from *Carmen*, though it burrowed through my head like some relentless worm. I keep holding up a cape and prot keeps goring me. How now brown cow?

I recalled in detail the previous day's session. We were coming closer and closer to the truth, but never quite getting there. Every opened door led to another empty room. How could I overcome the imperfections of a "kroladon" and get him to tell me what went on between prot (Robert) and a broken middle-aged man (his father) just before all hell literally broke loose? Perhaps I needed to sharpen the focus. Pound at that tiny interval of time just before little-boy prot ran away. Take it minute by minute, second by second until he reveals something about what happened. "*Tor-re-a-dor, en garrr-de!*"

Later that morning, while shivering on the back forty waiting for Cassandra to complete her meditations, I got a beep from Betty McAllister—my afternoon interview with a new patient had been cancelled. I immediately asked her to try to arrange an extra session with prot for that hour.

When I returned to the lawn, Cassie was gone. I didn't have time to track her down—there was a building committee meeting at ten o'clock. I took a stroll around the back forty, peering up at the open walls rising from the ground, the helmeted workers milling around above. What

were they thinking about? Lunch? A daughter's birthday?
Going home after work? A weekend football game? A trip
to K-PAX?

SESSION FORTY

W HILE WAITING for him to make an appearance I reviewed what I knew, exactly, about the moment before prot started running from the man he was bathing. All I really knew was that suddenly young prot was running away. What in God's name had happened at that seminal moment? Had something equally devastating happened to six-year-old Robert? And what was the connection between the two?

I had rescued a whole bowl of elderly bananas from the hospital kitchens. Prot went for them immediately, gobbling them down like a man starving. When he was finished and had sat back licking his fingers, I turned on the tape recorder and we went over the crucial events again without hypnosis. But he was unable to add a thing to fill in the brief gap in his memory. I uncovered the white dot and asked him to hypnotize himself. When he was in his usual deep trance I took him back to age sixty-eight and asked him to recall the details surrounding his bathing the broken, middle-aged dremer. He could barely remember the episode, and the only thing new I could get out of him was that the man started to rise from the hollow log (bath tub) just before prot departed the scene.

"Try to remember, prot! Was he reaching out to touch you? To grab you?"

"I— I don't— He was trying to—"

"Yes? What was he trying to do?"

"He was trying to *hit* me!"

"Why? Do you know why he was trying to hit you?"

"I— I— I—"

"Yes? Yes?"

"I can't remember. *I can't remember! I CAN'T REMEM-BER! DO YOU UNDERSTAND?*"

"All right, prot, calm down. Just relax. That's right. Relax. Good. Good. . . ."

He took several deep breaths. I brought him out of hypnosis and he was immediately in complete control again, as if nothing had happened.

I decided to try a different approach. "Space travel is somewhat risky, isn't it?" I ventured.

A familiar look of exasperation mixed with condescension crept over his face. "Gene, gene, gene. Didn't you have a bicycle when you were young?"

I suddenly remembered my father running alongside my new bike, finally pushing me off, my feeling of pride when I wiggled my way down the driveway by myself. "Yes. Yes, I did."

"Space travel to us is like riding a bicycle would be to you. Did you worry about falling down every time you jumped onto it?"

"Not after the first few tries."

162

"Egg-zack-a-tickly."

"Tell me—what's it like flying through empty space at several times the speed of light?"

"Like nothing."

"You mean there's nothing like it."

"No, I mean there's no sensation at all."

"Is it like being unconscious? Or asleep? Something like that?"

"Something like that. It may be akin to what you call 'hypnosis'."

I didn't miss the irony here, but there was no time to dwell on it. "No feeling of hunger or thirst, of getting any older. No sensation of any kind."

"Nope."

"Why don't you burn up in the atmosphere, like a meteor?"

"Same reason light doesn't burn up in the atmosphere."

"When you 'landed,' didn't you stop with a bit of a jolt?"

"No."

"How do you stop?"

"Simple, if you have the right program."

"You mean it's done by computer?"

"Of course."

"You bring a computer along wherever you go?"

"Sure. So do you. We're all basically computers with legs, haven't you noticed?"

"Are you saying the whole thing is programmed into your brain and you have no control over it?"

"Once the matrix is in place, it's a done deal."

"It overrides your own will power, is that it?"

"There's no such thing as 'will power,' my friend." He sounded rather wistful about this, I thought.

"We're all just a bag of chemicals, is that what you mean? No one has any control over his actions."

"Can hydrogen and oxygen stop themselves from making water?"

"You're talking about predestination."

"No, but you can call it that if it helps you to understand. I'm not saying your life is predetermined from beginning to end, only that in any given situation you will act in a predictable way, which is determined by the chemistry of your brain. You dig?"

"So if, say, a person killed his father, it's not his fault, right?"

"Of course not."

"Have you discussed this with Rob?"

"Many times."

"Then why does he feel guilty about his father's death?"

"He's a human being, ain't he?"

I stared at him for a moment. "Prot, something just occurred to me."

"Bully for you, doctor brewer."

"Did your whole body make the journey from K-PAX? Or just your 'spirit' or some sort of 'essence'?"

"Do I look like a ghost to you, doc?"

The tape indicates someone tapping furiously on a notepad with a ballpoint pen. "Then why—oh, the hell with it. Just a few more questions about your first trip to Earth, okay?"

"I'll save you some time. Though there was no sensation of growing older during the journey, I aged about seven of your months. The trip was uneventful, I didn't run into anything, I landed safely, took a look at the beings in china, attended a funeral in montana, commiserated with robert, the details of which you have ample notes and recordings, and made it back to K-PAX in one piece. Anything else?"

"Yes. Do all K-PAXians have this ability to pursue someone clear across the galaxy at a moment's notice?"

"Of course."

"Quite a talent."

"Not at all. Bear in mind that our species is several billion years ahead of yours. You'd be surprised at what you can learn just by sticking around long enough. Besides that, information is coming in all the time on every wavelength. The UNIVERSE is full of interesting vibes if you know how to listen."

"And without a moment's hesitation you vibed right across the galaxy to him."

"Right into the mortuary. Ugly word, don't you think?"

"What happened after the funeral?"

"We went to his house."

"What did he do after you got there?"

"He lay down on his bed and stared at the ceiling."

"Could you talk to him?"

"I could, but he didn't feel much like talking back."

"You came all the way from K-PAX and he wouldn't talk to you?"

"Nope. But it didn't matter."

"Why not?"

"After watching him for a while, I knew exactly how he was feeling."

"How? Had the same thing happened to you?"

His eyes rolled up and his fingers came together. At last he said, "K-PAXians can sense what's bothering another being."

"You can read minds?"

"Not exactly. It's difficult to explain. . . ."

"Try me."

He paused for another moment. "You could call it advanced semiotics. It's a combination of things—facial expression, subtle changes of color, especially in the UV range, tone of voice, body language, eye movements, frequency of swallowing, breathing pattern, smell, and—uh—a few other things."

"What things?"

"Oh, taste, smoothness of skin, pH, the kinds of radiation being given off, stuff like that. You feel exactly what the other being is feeling."

"You're an empath?"

"That's awfully *Star Trek*, coach, but—yes, all K-PAXians are what you call 'empaths.' It's easy when you don't consider yourself the center of the UNIVERSE."

"You think 'aps' are empathic, prot?"

"Sure. Just like most other beings. Have you ever tried to put anything over on a dog?"

He was right about that. Our Dalmatians somehow sensed what we were up to even before we did.

"And that's why you seem to understand the patients' problems better than their own doctors do."

"You could too if you could get outside your prison."

"Prison?"

"You know—the confines of your assumptions and beliefs."

Once again we seemed to have detoured. But suddenly I had another inspiration, a great one this time. "With all your marvelous insight into human nature, do you know what's bothering Robert right now?"

My excitement evidently came through loud and clear, because he chuckled before replying, "No."

"Why not?"

"Because I don't know where he is!"

"Well, can't you communicate with him somehow? Send out a signal on his 'wavelength' or something? Isn't he sending out some 'vibes'?"

"Nope. He doesn't seem to want any help."

"Damn it, prot, he's right there with you somewhere!"

"If he is, I don't see him. Do you?"

Of course I did, but he would never believe it. "All right. Let's go back to when you were sixty-eight point six. Somehow you helped young Robert get over his loss. How did you do that?"

"I told him the facts of life."

"You mean—"

"Nah, not that. About how the UNIVERSE works."

"What good did that do?"

"It seemed to make him feel better."

"How?"

"I explained to him that death is nothing to fear, that time will eventually reverse itself and that his father will live again."

"I see. And did he believe that?"

"Why shouldn't he? It's as true as my sitting here."

"So if you wanted to help Robert now, you'd just remind him that his father is not really dead, that he will live again in a few billion years—something like that?"

"He already knows that. But he's probably figured out the corollary."

"What corollary?"

He shook his head. "Hel-LO-o! That everything else that's happened to him would repeat itself as well."

Another brainstorm (which turned out to be another puny sprinkle) rumbled through my head. "Then do you have any suggestion as to what might help him? If we can find him, that is?"

"A trip to K-PAX would do him a WORLD of good."

"Would that help him forget—"

"No, but he would soon realize that nothing that happened to him here could ever happen there. Besides, he could actually see and talk to his father whenever he wanted to."

The hair on the back of my neck was tingling again. "What? How?"

"Now, gene, I told you about the—uh—what you call 'holograms' a long time ago."

"Oh. That." Tap, tap, tap. "So you would be willing to take Rob back with you when you go?"

"He got the first invitation—remember?"

"Why didn't he go with you the last time, do you suppose?" I asked him smugly. "Didn't he believe you?"

"There's something he wants to get off his chest first."

Unforgivably, I was becoming frustrated and annoyed. "Why doesn't he *do* it, then?" I shouted.

"Do what?"

"Get it off his chest, goddamn it!"

"Calm down, doc. Just relax. Good. Good. . . . He can't."

"Why not?"

"It's too terrible."

"Do you know what it is that's so terrible?"

"Haven't got a clue."

"I have! I've got a clue! I just need him to fill in a few details! Will you tell him that?"

"If I see him."

"I'm going to need your help on this, prot."

"If you can find him I'll speak to him."

"Thank you *so* much."

"It's the least I can do."

I tried to stay calm. "One last question: if everything is predestined, what's the point of living?"

"What's the point if it's not?"

Drained dry again, I watched him saunter out. Maybe, I thought, I should just ask him directly to tell me everything he knows about Rob that I don't. At least he couldn't come up later with some revelation and claim I never asked him about it. What the hell happened to prot's/Robert's father in that log/bathtub? Whatever it was, it was predestined, in prot's mind. The best way I know to alleviate a major guilt complex.

I ran into Carl Beamish in the restroom. Standing there side by side we heard a distant noise that sounded like a crowd at a basketball game. Memories of sweat and locker rooms and shiny gymnasium floors popped into my head. Karen never missed a game those four years I played on the high-school team. How I wished my father could have been there, even once. Might there be some sort of parallel universe, I mused, where different outcomes and missed opportunities come to be?

"Too much coffee?" Beamish opined, apparently noting that I was still standing at the urinal long after he had finished. Before I could reply another roar came from outside. I asked him what he made of it. "Maybe," he suggested, "prot has gone out to talk to the people at the front gate."

I was already late for my session with Linus, but I made a mental note to press Goldfarb on the preposterous situation in front of the hospital as soon as I found time. If I did, of course, she would probably appoint me chair of a committee of one to look into it.

"Doesn't that circus out there bother you at all?" I asked Beamish.

He looked at me as if I were crazy. "I only hope he has room to take me along, too!"

I had invited Giselle to lunch. When she finally arrived in the dining room I demanded that she tell me what was going on at the front gate.

"You should come and see for yourself, Dr. B!"

"Why won't they leave?"

"Most of them do go away after he talks to them, but more keep coming. There must be a couple thousand people out there right now. Some are bringing their dogs and cats to get a look at prot. And when he starts to speak there isn't a single bark or meow. It's absolutely quiet."

"I thought I heard cheers this morning."

"He always gets that when he tells them the Earth can be a K-PAX if we want it to be."

"That's it?"

"What more can he say?"

"I heard two cheers."

"The last one was when he was finished and went back inside."

"Go get your lunch."

By the time she got back I had already eaten my cottage cheese and crackers. Now I had to watch as she ate her mound of food. Fortunately, I had a one o'clock meeting.

"Giselle, I don't have much time. What did you learn from Rob's mother?"

She opened a manila envelope, which contained a set of snapshots, mainly of Rob's father, a few with the whole family. Most were taken when little Robin was only a baby. Gerald Porter was a big, robust man then. There was one of him in the slaughterhouse where he worked, wearing a bloody rubber apron. The later pictures were quite different. By the end of his life he had lost most of his muscle tissue. His face was drawn, there were dark circles around his eyes, his expression was that of someone trying to pretend he wasn't in pain, at least for the photos. His clothes were several sizes too big, mostly corduroy trousers and blue denim shirts. His thick black hair was parted on the right, I noted. "No home movies," she said, "but these are pretty revealing."

"I'll pass them on to Fred. What about his voice?"

"His mother said he used to be a deep baritone. Sang in the church choir. Toward the end it became rather squeaky, tired, high-pitched. He almost never slept, she told me. Couldn't eat much, either."

"The pain?"

"Terrible."

"What about Rob's relationship with his father? Did she notice anything unusual about it? Did she see any changes in him after his father came back from the hospital?"

"We didn't get into all that. Maybe you should talk to her yourself."

I stopped by my actor son's East Village apartment that evening to deliver the folder and discuss a timeframe for his visit to the hospital. The buzzer at the stoop elicited no response but the lock was broken so I went on up and tapped on the door. No answer. Disappointed, I searched my pockets for a pen. While I was writing Fred a note, a wiry man with a long gray ponytail showed up. I considered giving the package to him, but decided against it. He sidled into an apartment across the barely-lit hall, where he was greeted with a hug by another man wearing only shorts and an undershirt. The wall was cracked even worse than the one on Fred's side. I slid the folder under the door, along with a request to call me, and grabbed a taxi to Grand Central.

The following day, Thursday, I happened to glance into the quiet room and spotted Ophelia. There was something noticeably different about her, but I couldn't put my finger on it. Alex was there too, busily consulting an encyclopedia, an atlas, and a gazetteer. Ophelia waved. Usually she pretends not to see me, fearing I might judge her too harshly about something or another, I suppose. I motioned for her to step outside so we wouldn't bother Alex.

"How are you today, Ophie?"

"I think I'm cured. How are *you*?"

"Ophelia! What happened?"

"I'm not afraid anymore."

"That's right!" I heard Alex shout.

"Why not?"

"Prot ordered me not to think of a rabbit."

I had to smile. "And you did."

She giggled. "I didn't mean to. I couldn't help it."

Alice appeared from behind a sofa, spotted us, and dashed from the room squeaking like a mouse.

"So you disobeyed his command."

"Yes."

"And now you think you're cured."

"Yes. No, I take that back. I *know* I am."

She still wasn't well, of course. She couldn't have made that much progress in several months of analysis, let alone a few minutes with prot. "That's great, Ophie. I guess we'll have to take up your case in the staff meeting next Monday."

"No need to do that. I've already been assigned to Ward One."

"Ward One? Who assigned you to Ward One?"

"Prot did."

"Correct!" Alex called out.

"Ophelia! You know prot doesn't run the hospital!"

"Of course I know that. But the order was countersigned by Dr. Goldfarb!"

The afternoon lecture was another bust. I had long ago given up following the syllabus I had drawn up at the beginning of the year (actually more like twenty years ago) and, as had become my habit, I began by briefing the students on my lack of progress in finding Robert, adding something about Ophelia and the other patients prot had managed to help in one way or another. "Oliver Sacks," naturally, turned the discussion back to prot. "Maybe you could get him to speak to us," he suggested. "You know—tell us what he's learned about the patients and how we can better deal with them ourselves."

I might have reminded him that he didn't have any patients yet. Instead, I barked, "He's not here to teach a bunch of medical students how to become psychiatrists. In any case, I don't think the world is ready to be treated by a clone of prot 'disciples,' do you?"

"I don't know. All I'm suggesting is that we could listen to what he has to say and see if we can learn anything from it. Draw our own conclusions."

"Sorry."

From around the room came roars and mutterings.

"All right, all right! I'll tell you what I'll do. I'll get him to jot down a few of his thoughts about the patients, and I'll bring them next time. Assuming he agrees to do so. Fair enough?"

Oliver wasn't finished. Oliver is never finished. "Ask him also what he *doesn't* understand about them. I think that would tell us a lot about *him*."

"That is correct!" someone piped up.

Reluctantly I agreed, and abruptly changed the subject. "We're going to end the hour by talking a little bit about sexual deviation."

For once I had their full attention—even prot seemed forgotten for the moment.

SESSION FORTY-ONE

PROT FELL into a trance immediately. "Okay, prot, please unhypnotize yourself."

"What—" He stared bug-eyed around the room. "Where am I?"

"All right, we'll dispense with the comedy today."

"My dear sir, I don't think you'd know comedy if it rose up and bit you on the hiney." He reached for a cluster of red grapes and stuffed them into his maw, stems and all, along with a hunk of ripe peach.

"I'm willing to agree with that if you'll tell me something I don't know about Rob."

Prot laughed heartily, like a little boy who's discovered something silly. His mouth was a rainbow of color. "I was wrong, doctor b. You *do* have a sense of humor."

"You mean you're not going to divulge even one of his little secrets?"

"No, I mean there are a million things you don't know about rob. Or anyone else, including yourself."

"Then it should be easy for you. Fill me in. What are some things I don't know about Rob?"

"Well, for example, you don't even know that he tried to commit suicide on at least two occasions."

"He what? When?"

"After his wife and daughter were killed—remember?"

"Of course I do. He tried to drown himself in the river behind his house."

"Very good! But what about the first time—do you know about that?"

"What first time?"

"When he was six and a half. He tried to hang himself in his room."

"At *six*?"

"Actually, he was closer to seven. To be precise, he was six years, ten months, nine days—"

"And that's when he first called you? After the suicide attempt?"

"By george, I think you've finally got it."

"He called you because he didn't want to die."

Prot pushed another bunch of grapes into his mouth. "No, my human friend, he called me because he *failed* to die."

"You knew this and never told me? There are a few things you don't understand about human beings yourself, my alien friend."

"I already know more than I want to."

"Please," I implored (it came out more like a whine), "let's not debate that issue today. Just tell me why Rob wanted to kill himself."

"Because his father died."

"But there wasn't anything he could do about it, was there?"

"He thought it was his fault."

"Why was it his fault?"

"I don't know. You'll have to ask *him*."

"Goddammit, prot, he won't talk to me!"

"Maybe you've been asking him the wrong questions."

"I haven't asked him anything," I shot back. "He's not here, *remember*?"

"If you had asked the right things in the first place, maybe he would be!"

It was all I could do not to explode. Instead, I tapped my yellow pad rather vigorously with my pen. "Do you have any suggestions about what the right questions might be?"

Prot gazed at me as if I were a complete idiot. "Well, you might try to find out how his father died, for example."

"But—he died of natural causes, didn't he? Resulting from a work-related injury suffered months earlier, as I remember."

"Did you read the death certificate?"

"No. Did you?"

"Nope."

"Then how do you know how he died?"

"What do you get when you add two and two?"

"I suppose you're going to tell me the answer is five."

"It depends on what dimension you're in."

"Are you trying to tell me that two and two are five in Rob's case?"

"Only that you might try looking at the situation from a different angle."

177

"What if I don't know what angle to look at the situation from?"

"Well, I suppose you could re-examine your educational system. . . ."

"You mean my training as a psychiatrist?"

"No, dear boy, I mean your training as a perceptive being. Of course it might take you a few thousand years."

"Prot, we don't *have* a few thousand years."

"Give or take a few decades."

"Prot, I'm asking you flat out to tell me anything you know that I don't know."

"You have a rutad hanging out of your nose."

"A what?"

"A bugger."

"Oh." He watched with some amusement as I took out my handkerchief and removed the offending particle. "Is that all you have to say?"

"About your proboscis?"

"Or anything else."

"For the time being."

"All right. We're going to change the subject."

"Back to 'uncles,' I suppose."

"Maybe. There are still a few questions I want to ask you about your childhood on K-PAX."

"Will they be relevant this time, gino?"

"Let me decide that."

He shrugged. "Decide away."

"Thank you. All right. I'm going to ask you something about the time you were a baby on K-PAX. Less than twenty years old. Anything happen to you during that first twenty years that was unpleasant for you in any way?"

He scratched his head, for all the world like an ordinary human being. It's always fascinated me that trying to recall some obscure fact causes one's scalp to itch. "Not really. Pretty routine babyhood."

"All right. Let's shift to a later time. You're exactly fifty-five years old. Do you have a pet?"

"We don't have pets on K-PAX."

"Well, is there anything that follows you around? Goes where you go? Any animals that are around more than others?"

"There was a folgam that hung around sometimes."

"What's a 'folgam'?"

"Something like a cat, only smaller."

I was jolted by the recollection that five-year-old Robin's pedophilic Uncle Dave secured his silence by killing a kitten (and a stray dog), and threatening to do the same to him. "Cat?"

"See ay tee. Cat."

"But cats are carnivores, aren't they?"

"Not on K-PAX."

"A vegetarian cat."

"I just said that, *nicht wahr*?"

"You said there 'was' a folgam. What happened to it?"

"He wasn't an 'it.' He was a 'he.'"

"What happened to him?"

Prot frowned and pressed his lips together. "He went off somewhere."

"He disappeared?"

"No, he wasn't of the Cheshire variety. He just went away."

"And you don't know where."

"That's it!"

"You woke up one morning and he was gone."

"Correct! Except we don't have 'morning' in the sense you mean it. You see, with our two suns—"

"All right, all right. What happened after the folgam went away?"

"Not much. I went to a library and retrieved some information about folgams."

"Why?"

"I wondered whether they always went away like that."

"You missed your folgam, didn't you, prot?"

"He wasn't 'my' folgam. I was just curious."

"Did you ever have another folgam follow you around?"

He checked his fingernails. "No."

"Was anyone else around when your folgam ran away?"

He considered this. "Off in the distance I saw someone, but I couldn't tell who it was."

"Too far away?"

"Yes."

"Was he fat or thin?"

"He seemed to be rather heavy for a dremer."

"You hadn't seen him before?"

"I told you—I couldn't tell who he was."

"Okay. Now let's return to the time you were sixty-eight. Remember? You woke up with a headache and all the rest?"

He nodded suspiciously.

"Before this happened you were bathing someone, right?"

He nodded again.

"Was he 'a little heavy for a dremer'?"

"No."

"So it wasn't the same being you saw after your—the folgam ran off."

"Nope."

"Do you know who he was?"

"Yes, I do."

"You do?" I could feel my heart beginning to pound. "What was his name?"

"I don't know."

"Do you know your father's name?"

"As far as I know, I never met my father."

"Well, what kind of relationship did you have with the dremer in the hollow log?"

"The usual. We talked about various things, looked at the stars, admired the korms."

"What did you talk about in particular?"

"A lot of things."

"Sex?"

"That's not something that comes up very often on K-PAX. There isn't that much to say about it."

"Did he—uh—demonstrate any sexual activity toward you?"

"Of course not! Why should he?"

"But you had seen him before."

"Many times."

"Anything unusual happen on those occasions?"

"No."

"So tell me—why were you bathing him?"

"Haven't we been over this?"

"Not in any detail."

"All of a sudden you're a detail man?"

"That's right!"

"I was cleaning him because he couldn't clean himself."

"Why not?"

"He couldn't move his arms and legs very well."

"They were injured?"

"I doubt it. We have ways to repair people who are injured."

"What was his problem, then?"

"I don't know."

"Was he in any pain?"

"Yes."

"Didn't you give him something for that? Some balnok bark to chew on, for example?"

"It didn't do him much good."

"I see. And had you ever cleaned this man before?"

"No."

"All right. You say you had seen this dremer many times. How long had you known him?"

"For a while."

"Why is that? Don't K-PAXians move around a lot?"

"He couldn't walk very well. So he didn't move around much."

"What about yourself? Didn't you move around a lot? Leave him behind?"

"Children don't move around as much as adults. Anyway, we seemed to be going in the same direction most of the time."

"So you saw him fairly often?"

"More often than most beings, I suppose. So what?"

"But you don't know his name."

"I already told you that!" he snapped.

"After you hit your head on something and lost your memory, you never saw him again—right?"

"Never."

"Why not?"

"Who knows? I suppose he finally moved on."

"Could he have died?"

This seemed to jolt prot for a second. But he said, simply, "It's possible, of course."

"How old was he?"

"Four hundred or so, I suppose."

"Pretty young for a K-PAXian."

"Just approaching middle age."

"Does anyone ever die at that age on K-PAX?"

"Hardly ever."

"But it's possible."

"Yes, it's possible! What isn't?"

"Prot, I want you to think about this next question before you give me an answer. Could the man have been your father?"

"I doubt it," he replied without hesitation.

"Why not?"

"I've never met my father."

"You're lying, aren't you, prot?"

"Moi? I told you: I've never told a lie in my life."

"K-PAXians have a lot of different talents, don't they? I think one of them is to lie convincingly enough to fool everyone else. Is that possible?"

"Anything's— I mean, of course it's *possible*, but it doesn't happen to be true."

"You know who your father is, don't you? Or at least you suspect who he is."

"I've told you time and again that I don't!"

"And you lied about it time and again, didn't you?"

"No! I didn't!"

"The man in the hollow log is your father, isn't he?"

"No! I mean . . . I don't know who my father is, don't you understand that? It's a simp—"

"But it's *possible* that the man in the log is your father, isn't it?"

"YES, IT'S POSSIBLE, GODDAMN IT!"

I swiveled away. "Thank you, prot. That's all for today." I busied myself with my notes. A few seconds later I peeked around, but he was already gone. How now, brown prot? Maybe our educational system sucks, but it seems to be getting us somewhere, *nicht wahr*? In another few years of badgering, I assured myself, I may be able to get to the bottom of all this!

But there were only a few weeks left, not enough time to get even halfway down. With the hourglass rapidly draining, should I focus all my remaining time and attention on Rob himself, press him on what it was he wanted to "get off his chest"? Was it to confess a role in his beloved father's death, as I was beginning to suspect?

I sought out Giselle and found her in the lounge, sitting in Frankie's favorite window seat, the very spot where former patient Howie, some seven and a half years earlier, had sought out "the bluebird of happiness." I asked her what she was contemplating.

"Oh, Dr. B, I was just thinking about all the people we'll be leaving behind. Look at Alex over there, trying to be someone he's not. He's wasting his life, and it's too precious for that. And all the other patients. Most of them don't even know what they're unhappy *about*. Or who live in fear but aren't sure what they're afraid *of*. We can't take them *all* with us. It's sad, isn't it?"

I refrained from observing how sad her own dream would be when it ended. Instead, I told her about the brief conversation I had had the previous evening with Rob's mother. "Robin and his father were very close when he was six, and they spent all their time together the summer he died. His dad called him 'Robbie'—I'll mention that to Fred. Another thing I found out was that the man was incontinent. He even wore a diaper, like a baby! And one other thing might be relevant: because of all the hospital bills, the family was going to lose the house. He was pretty distraught about that."

"The house? Why?"

"Because they couldn't make the payments. On all of his medical bills, either. They were in pretty bad shape, financially. I think that's why prot's so down on the free-enterprise system!"

"But they *didn't* lose the house, did they?"

"No. He had some life insurance. Not much, but enough to keep the creditors away for a while."

Giselle thought about this for a moment. "What did Rob's mom know about—uh—"

"Not much. The girls were already in their room, asleep. She heard a commotion and went to see what had happened. She found her husband in the bathtub. He was already dead by then. She thought he died of a heart attack. Prot isn't so sure. Can you get a copy of the death certificate?"

She nodded, emitted a huge sigh, and slouched toward the door.

Before leaving the lounge I stopped alongside Alex, who

was sitting in the big overstuffed chair in the corner paging through the huge encyclopedia, taking notes onto a yellow tablet identical to one of my own. A visitor might have thought he was one of the staff, hard at work researching a difficult patient's problems. "Hello, Alex, how's it going?"

"Almost ready," he replied *sotto voce*, without looking up.

"Keep up the good work," I murmured, half to myself. It wasn't until I had left the room that I realized he had responded in a most unAlex-like manner. Of course! I thought. Until he spoke to prot, no one had ever given him a chance to actually *be* who he wanted to be, a deeply felt desire haunting most people, even those outside these walls. I wondered whether this would work for some of the other patients. What if we catered to their whims? Gave them a chance to actually be who they wanted to be, at least for a little while?

The morning was taken up by a visit from the popular "TV shrink," who had cancelled a similar appearance two years earlier. He was a roly-poly, apple-cheeked little man, someone who would make the perfect Santa Claus. A farmer by trade, he smelled faintly of manure. I wondered what my former patient Chuck would have thought of him.

He had been scheduled for the whole day, but once again had to cancel the afternoon portion because of certain unspecified but pressing engagements. Though I was secretly glad because I had more than enough work to attend to, his seeming arrogance annoyed me, just as it had in 1995.

But perhaps this had more to do with the fact that his books (unlike my own) have made him a wealthy man. Nevertheless, I was looking forward to meeting him because one can always learn something about communicating with one's patients from a colleague who does it so effectively on a nationwide scale.

The first thing he said, when Thorstein (who picked him up at Penn Station—he doesn't fly) escorted him into my office, was, "Life is like false teeth." I had no idea what that meant but I nodded wisely, not wanting to start off our relationship by seeming dense.

I offered the famed guru some coffee. Wagging a pudgy finger, he iterated, "You build a house one card at a time!" Assuming this to be an affirmative response, I buzzed one of the secretaries to bring us some. While we were waiting I asked him where he had studied. "A grain of sand is worth more than all the handwriting on the wall," he declared with a twinkle. (I found out later he hadn't gotten past the eighth grade.)

I tried to shift the conversation to something less personal. "How do you like New York?"

"The bigger the goose, the smaller the gander!" he shouted, pounding his fist on my desk. This went on for half an hour, and I was quite relieved when Thorstein arrived to take him away.

A makeshift seminar was set up for eleven o'clock, disrupting the schedules of staff and patients alike. Nevertheless, it was quite well attended. I won't present a verbatim transcript of that discussion; suffice it to say it was a continuous litany of aphorisms, homilies, nursery rhymes, Biblical quotations, and old wives' tales, commencing with "What is a lie, but the truth in disguise?" and ending with "You can catch more flies with honey than you can with vinegar, but vinegar is cheaper." Unfortunately there was no time for questions, but he was rewarded with a generous round of applause as he hurried out the door to his "pressing engagement."

At lunch afterward, though no one could argue about anything the great philosopher had said, neither could anyone tell me why life is like false teeth.

Lose a few, win a few. The meeting with Linus turned out to be a breakthrough. I merely asked him why he felt it necessary to check over his room exactly thirty-seven times before he could leave it, a question I'm sure I have put to him a dozen times before. In any case the answer, same as always, was, "So that I don't make any more mistakes."

I suppressed a yawn. "Mistakes like what?"

"Like I did on that paper. You know, the one about the DNA sequence of one of the taste genes."

"You mean you made the mistake of using the wrong data when you wrote it up for publication?"

"No, I mean I should have selected a gel that wasn't so obviously a phony."

Had Linus been talking with prot? I sat up straighter. "You're *admitting* you cheated on that? You fudged the data?"

"I fudged *all* my data."

"You—but why? Everyone I've talked to and the reports I've read all say that you have a brilliant mind and could easily plan meaningful experiments and come up with significant and important results."

"That's true."

"So why screw around with the data? Wouldn't it be easier just to do the experiments?"

"I hate doing experiments."

"You hate—then why did you go into molecular biology?"

"Dr. Brewer, have you met my parents?"

"Yes, I have. They're top scientists, both of them. That alone should have given you a leg up on everyone else."

"But neither of them ever asked me what I wanted to do with my life. They both assumed I would follow in their formidable footsteps. They never even asked for my opinion, and if I tried to give one, they ignored it. One thing led inexorably to another—what could I do?"

I understood his dilemma. In fact, I identified with him. I almost *empathized* with him. My own father had assumed I wanted to follow in his footsteps. Who knows—if left to my own devices, I may have anyway. The point is I didn't seem to get a vote in the matter. I even felt obligated to follow his wishes long after he was dead!

I asked Linus what he would do with his life if he could start all over again.

"I'd like to be a cowboy," he told me with the straightest face I had ever seen. I felt as though I were being watched by a dog and it was suppertime.

"Maybe something can be done about that."

He actually crawled over to me, wrapped his arms around my ankles, and cried. The truth is, I joined him. I brushed down his hair and wept for him, for myself, for all of us.

*   *   *

Freddy came to dinner on Sunday. (We had invited the ballerina, too, but she couldn't make it. A good thing, though—he ate enough for two people.) Although he had auditioned for a number of parts he was still without employment, except for a little drama coaching at one of the city's high schools. He seemed a trifle down, and acted as if there were something he wanted to tell us. The last time it was giving up flying—was he becoming disillusioned with his acting career? It certainly seemed a poorly-paid profession. Or was he worried, like most of us, about being a failure at what he did? Whatever it was, he kept it bottled up inside in typical Fred fashion.

I gave him all the information we had about Robert's father, and I could see him mulling it over, forming some sort of characterization in his mind. In the end we scheduled a "dress rehearsal" for the following Saturday. He would come to the house in some old baggy clothes and we would go over the setup and what to expect when he came to the hospital, a visit we planned for the following week. I realized, with no little regret, that he had never been to my office.

We watched a ballet on TV that afternoon. Was Fred so attentive because he was trying to please me? Or was it simply that he had learned a lot about the art from his roommate? Perhaps he was studying the dancers in order to increase his chances of landing a role on Broadway. Who would know? Who can get inside another person's head, even that of someone close to us? Only his mother seemed completely happy, humming away in the kitchen. She disliked ballet, and wasn't going to pretend otherwise. Karen has always been exactly who she is, nothing more, nothing less. And, in her case at least, that's quite enough.

SESSION FORTY-TWO

THE MONDAY morning staff meeting was a halcyon affair, with Linus's transfer to Ward One in process and Milton, who had been in other institutions for more than three decades before coming to MPI, about to be discharged altogether. Carried away by the general good feeling, I contemplated the perfect copy of Van Gogh's *Sunflowers*, painted by a former patient, and nibbled on a cinnamon donut, knowing I would regret it later on when I stepped on the scales. I rationalized this by professing that I would be quite willing to have a cinnamon donut every time a patient is discharged.

"You'd better start stocking up, then," Beamish roared, "because I've got someone else who's ready for Ward One, in my opinion."

I stared at the tiny glasses, which weren't much bigger than his eyes. "Who?—Ophelia?"

"That's right! How did you know?"

"I've noticed some changes."

Menninger agreed. "She's like a different person."

"Maybe she *is* a different person," I suggested, not knowing what the hell I was talking about.

"Whoever she is, she's no longer psychotic," Beamish assured us. "I can't even get a good neurosis out of her anymore."

Goldfarb looked around the room. "Any dissenters?"

There were none.

"Let's get rid of her!" she exclaimed, flinging her pen onto the big mahogany table. A crude expression, perhaps, but it's one of Goldfarb's favorites, something of a talisman, I suppose. "Anyone else ready for Ward One?"

"I think Don and Joan are ready, as long as they go together," Chang replied. "It's wonderful—between the two of them they seem to make a whole human being."

"Same with Alice and Albert," Goldfarb chipped in, "though they're probably not ready to move down yet. But we should give prot the credit for putting them together."

That was true in the latter case, but it was I who had first thought of pairing "Don Knotts" and "Joan of Arc," though at this point who would have believed me? I did manage to point out that there were some patients who didn't seem to be affected much by prot's visit—Frankie, Cassandra, the autists, the deviates, the psychopaths.

"Give him time," said Menninger. "Give him time. Cassie, at least, has broken out of her depression. Maybe prot had something to do with that." I replied rather sheepishly that I would speak to her about it.

In view of all the upcoming vacancies in Ward Two there was room for a group of new patients waiting to make the move from "the big institute" (at Columbia) to MPI. "Let's bring them over early," Chang proposed. "Let prot have a crack at them before he goes." Mine was the only dissenting vote.

The meeting wound up with a discussion of the annual outing to the Metropolitan Museum of Art. It was set for Monday, the fifteenth, when the venerable institution is normally closed. We would have the place all to ourselves (I suspect this gesture on the part of the museum staff was more for the benefit of their paying patrons than for our patients, but it was nonetheless appreciated).

"What's going on with the new wing?" Thorstein demanded. "I was on the lawn this morning and there doesn't seem to be much happening." Everyone looked at me accusingly.

"I spoke to the foreman last week. It's got something to do with the holidays and with a union vote and something else I didn't quite get. He doesn't speak much English."

"No problem," Goldfarb said with a smirk. "At this rate, we're not going to need the damn thing anymore." Goldfarb had made a joke! She lifted her pen. "Anything else?"

I mentioned the crowd at the front gate, which seemed to be getting bigger every day.

"What's the big deal?" Thorstein wanted to know. "They seem to be an orderly bunch. All they want is a word from prot. Anyway, the fault lies with you."

I found myself hoping he would be successful in finding a position elsewhere. "*Moi?*"

"If you hadn't written those books, no one would know he was here."

"What are they going to do when he leaves?" mused Beamish.

"The question is, what are *we* going to do when he leaves?" Goldfarb muttered, deadly serious again.

I found Betty waiting for me in my office. She seemed nervous, even agitated. I asked her where the disturbance was.

"Right here," she wailed.

"What do you mean?"

"I've got an appointment in an hour to have a root canal done."

"So?"

"I'm afraid of the drill."

Betty's teeth have never been very good. Now I knew why. "What is it about the drill that bothers you?"

"I'm afraid it's going to get loose and shoot through my skull."

"Betty! The odds against that are astronomical!"

Her hands were picking away at each other. "I know. But it doesn't help."

I could see she was terrified. "Well, do you want me to recommend someone to help you get through this?"

"I— Maybe. I thought you could just say something real quick that would do it."

"Nothing is that easy in this business, Betty—you know that. How did you get through the previous visits to the dentist?"

"My husband always took me. But he can't go today."

I thought immediately of sending prot with her, but quickly rejected the idea. "I don't think this is something we can solve in an hour. Do you want to change the appointment until we can look into it a little more?"

"I can't. If I wait any longer she'll have to pull it, and that's worse."

At that moment my wife walked in. "Hi! I was in town today, and for some reason I found myself heading this way. I thought we might have lunch together. Hi, Betty—want to come with us?"

"I can't," she replied dismally.

"What's the matter?"

Betty repeated the whole story.

"I understand perfectly," Karen assured her. "I have the same problem. What time's your appointment? I'll go with you. Then we'll have a nice lunch somewhere."

As if a valve had opened, all the tension drained immediately from Betty's face. On their way out, Karen gave me a wave over her shoulder and a little smile that seemed to say, "See? It's easy if you empathize with your patients."

I didn't even know she had a problem with dentists.

I went to see for myself how Cassandra was doing. While I was looking for her on the lawn (she liked to be outside where she could contemplate the heavens, regardless of how cold it was) it occurred to me that perhaps she was a kind of autistic savant, someone who devotes so much of her mental capabilities to one single activity that she actually *can* see a pattern in events that the rest of us can't, and merely reaches some perfectly logical conclusion about the long-term results.

I found her sitting on her favorite bench in her old worn coat, her arms wrapped around her as if she were confined to a straightjacket. I waited for a few minutes while she tuned in to me.

"Hi, Cassie. How are you feeling?"

"Just fine." She even smiled a little.

"Good. I'm glad you're feeling better."

"Prot told me not to give up hope."

"About what?"

"About a trip to K-PAX. He says someone else might come back for me later on."

"Can we talk about that for a minute?"

"He's leaving on the thirty-first."

"Yes, I know. What I was wondering was, have you figured out who he's taking with him this time?"

"Not for sure. Only how many of us will get to go."

"Really? How many will there be?"

"Two."

"Only two?" I sniggered. "I thought he was supposed to take a hundred of us to K-PAX."

She glared at me through the hair falling over her eyes. "That's right. But only two of *us*."

"You mean the people who live here at the hospital."

"Yes."

"But you have no idea who they will be."

"Not yet," she sighed, turning back to the sky.

"Do you have any idea *when* you might know who he'll be taking with him?"

But she was already gone, lost in the stars.

On my way back to the big front door I reflected yet again on how little we know about the human mind. As if to prove my point, I ran into Alice and Albert coming out, accompanied by a couple of cats. The A's now seemed inseparable. "How are you two doing?" I inquired.

"Great!" Albert exclaimed, whipping out a tape measure.

"Alice's last 'big' phase was a full two centimeters short of the time before, which was two short of the one before that!"

Alice, brandishing a stopwatch, added, "And Albert was two minutes closer to estimating the duration of an hour than he was last week! Isn't it great?"

"Wonderful!" I said, and meaning it. "Keep it up!"

"In another month or two, we'll be cured!"

I wasn't so sure about that, but I doubted they would be among the lucky winners of an all-expenses-paid trip to K-PAX.

A dense crowd was still milling quietly about the front gate. Some of them glanced in occasionally to see who was on the lawn, but it wasn't prot, and they had no interest in the rest of the patients. Not surprising, actually, since most people feel the same way toward the mentally ill and, by and large, hope they'll just disappear. Unfortunately, so do the HMO's.

As I was leaving the hospital to give my "Principles of Psychiatry" lecture, Giselle stopped me in the corridor with an envelope addressed to "dr. eugene n. brewer, EARTH." Of course it was from prot, and it contained the list of things he did and did not understand about our patients (as well as the rest of us), which I had asked him to compile for the benefit of my students. I perused the "list," which was neatly typed on a 3x5 card:

what I know about homo sapiens
you've been brainwashed from the beginning—by your parents, your relatives, your neighbors, your schools, your

religions, your employers, your governments. no wonder you're such a mess.

what I don't understand about homo sapiens
how anyone can shoot a deer.

I stuck it back in the envelope. "Tell prot I'll pass this on. By the way, did you get a copy of Rob's father's death certificate?"

"Nope. They're still looking for it. I'll try to have it for you in time for tomorrow's session."

With that I headed for Columbia to face the wrath of my students. To my surprise, however, they took prot's microtreatise with great equanimity. In fact, as I proceeded to unload as much information as I could cram into the tiny hour, I didn't hear another word about him. It was as quiet as a funeral in there, but what they were all thinking about was anybody's guess.

Three more weeks! As I waited for prot to show up for our forty-second session together, I reflected on the death certificate, which had arrived only that morning. Rob's father had, in fact, died from "natural causes." There was no autopsy. The cause must have seemed obvious to the local doctor: a heart attack or massive stroke brought on by the unremitting stress of living inside a terribly battered body. Nothing very surprising there.

Without saying a word, prot sauntered in and grabbed up a handful of kiwis, which he noisily devoured.

"Prot, please relax now and feel free to put yourself—"

"I wish you'd make up your mind, doctor. Onetwo—"

"Thank you."

"What for?" he mumbled.

"Never mind. How do you feel?"

"Like I'm traveling on a beam of light."

"Good. Now just relax." Uncertain about whether he was under or just pretending, I checked his pulse: thirty-eight, about normal for the hypnotized prot. "Okay, prot, I'd like to speak to Robert for a minute."

Prot/Robert drooped into the usual slouch, but of course there was no sign of comprehension or movement. "Rob, it's me. Dr. Brewer. Gene. How are you feeling today?"

No response.

"Prot tells me you'd like to get something off your chest. Is that true?"

Not a sign of cognition.

"Well, I'm here. What is it you wanted to tell me?"

I waited for several minutes in case he was on the verge of responding. But there was no indication of any such attempt. "Rob, please listen to me. You don't have to say anything, but I want you to hear what I've got to tell you. If you can hear me, please nod."

There wasn't the slightest hint of movement.

"I know you can hear me, Rob. So just listen. I've got a theory about what happened when you were a boy and I'd like to run it by you, all right? If it's right, don't say anything [a sneaky trick, but sometimes one has to resort to them]. But if it's wrong, please let me know. Otherwise we'll be off on the wrong foot, heading in the wrong direction. Understand?"

No response.

"Think back for a moment to the summer of 1963 when

you were six and your father began telling you about the stars. Think of all the wonderful nights you spent gazing into the heavens with him out in the back yard. Remember he told you about the sun and the planets and comets and asteroids and meteors and so on, and how exciting that was? And then he told you about all the billions of stars in the sky, and how a lot of them could have solar systems like our own, and that there were probably intelligent beings on some of the planets out there? How they might be different from us but maybe not so different? And how we might be able to communicate with them and that it might even be possible some day to visit them or that we might have visitors from one of those faraway worlds? Remember how nice it was out in the yard on those warm summer nights with his arm around your shoulder? How you helped your father back into the house when it was time to go to bed? Then your mother tucked you in and kissed you and said goodnight? Wouldn't it be wonderful to be able to go back there and live that time over again? Even for a little while?"

Rob sat like a stone.

"But one night he soiled himself while you were outside and he needed to be cleaned up. Your mother was busy or wasn't feeling well, and she asked if you would help him with his bath just this once. You said you would, and supported him while he made his painful way to the bathroom. You helped him get undressed and into the tub—remember? You kicked his dirty clothes toward the hamper and began to wash him.

"But you were dirty too, so you got out of your pants and T-shirt. Then, while you were leaning over him, his hands began to grope for you. You didn't like what was happening. You remembered the time you were living with your aunt and uncle and everything you'd been trying to forget came back."

Rob seemed to fidget a little, and I think I heard a little choke.

"Not only did your father seem to be behaving like Uncle Dave, but at that moment you knew you could no longer depend on your 'friend and protector' to keep you from harm. *There was no one in the whole world you could trust!* You threw down the washcloth and ran out of the bathroom and into the back yard. Your dad fell back into the tub. You were so distressed that you kept running on into the woods behind the house. It was dark and you stumbled and fell and hit your head against a rock or a tree. You passed out, and when you finally woke up and decided you had better go back inside, you heard your mother screaming. Despite your splitting headache you ran in and found that your father had died after you left him in the tub. He was lying under the water. You were terribly confused. You thought it was your fault because he had fallen and, if you hadn't run away, he would still be alive. Isn't that right, Rob? Isn't that what happened when you were six?"

I watched him carefully but, except for the sound of heavy breathing, he didn't twitch a muscle.

"You never forgave yourself, did you, Rob? You were never able to shake the guilt and sorrow, were you? Rob, please tell me if I'm wrong about any of this."

I waited for quite a while but his breathing quieted and there was no further response.

"Then I can assume my theory is correct and that everything happened more or less as I described it. If not, please indicate this by blinking your eyes once."

His eyelids didn't flicker. But a tear rolled down his cheek!

"All right, Rob. In a moment I'm going to let you go back to where you were a little while ago. But I want you to think about something in the time between now and your next visit. I want you to know something you didn't know before. Your father's death was brought on by the extreme stress on his body resulting from the injury he had suffered months earlier at the slaughterhouse. It was sudden, but it could have happened at any time. He wasn't reaching for you, he was reaching *out*, already feeling the effects of whatever it was that killed him. Isn't that possible, Rob? You couldn't have done anything about it even if you had stayed with him. Do you understand? It wasn't your fault. It wasn't anyone's fault. On Earth people die sometimes, despite anything we might do. You didn't kill your father, Rob. If anything, you made his last few weeks some of the happiest of his life. You gave him something that he needed and wanted. You gave him your love."

Not a movement, not a whisper.

"All right, you can go now. I'll see you again in a few days. Think about what I've told you."

I waited another moment before saying, "Okay, prot, you can come on back now."

"Ehhh—what's up, doc?"

"Not a damn thing. Please unhypnotize yourself."

He complied immediately. Stifling a yawn, he said, "Hiya, gino. Did you find robert?"

"I think so, but I'm not sure."

"Wouldn't you recognize him if you saw him?"

"I'm not even sure about that."

He shook his head. "He looks a little like me. Except—"

"I know what he looks like!"

He jumped up. "Well, if we're through here, I'll just be on my way. . . ."

"Not so fast."

"You call this fast, earthling?"

"Did you hear anything I just said to Rob?"

"You think I would eavesdrop?"

"No. But it might've happened accidentally."

"Well, I never heard a word. You could have been talking to santa claus for all I know. Or any of your other mythical beings."

"Please sit down."

Prot plopped back into the vinyl chair.

"All right. I just wanted to tell you what you missed. I presented Rob with a theory about what happened to him when he was six. How his father died and how he reacted to it. Want to hear about it?"

"Why not? We've still got eleven minutes and thirty-eight seconds left."

I started to recap the highlights of my "conversation" with Robert, then had a better idea. I rewound the tape and played it for prot, who seemed fascinated by it. Afterward I forgot to turn the tape recorder back on for a few seconds, but, as I remember it, he said something like, "Your primitive methods never cease to amaze me."

"Damn it, prot, I'm not interested in your assessment of my technique or of the human race right now. What I'd like to know is whether you think my hypothesis is credible."

"Anything's—"

"Yes, I know, but is it *likely*?"

"I'd say no."

I remember rubbing my temples hard at this point, but the pain didn't go away. "Why not?"

"He didn't die of a heart attack, or any other 'natural' cause."

"He didn't? How do you know that?"

"I was there, remember?"

"But you didn't show up until the funeral, did you?"

"When I saw the body, I realized that what happened to rob's pa could only happen on EARTH. Never on K-PAX."

"What happened to him?"

"He drowned."

Suddenly I realized the full implication of what he was telling me. "Are you saying that Rob's father committed suicide?"

"Did I say that?"

"But how else—"

"Maybe it was an accident. Or maybe somebody done him in. To mention a couple of obvious possibilities." He stood up, flipped on his dark glasses, which made him look like an aging rock star, and sauntered out.

After he left I sagged down in my chair like a sack of excrement. I thought for a moment that this must be similar to what Robert felt. Then of course I realized he was feeling much worse than I could possibly even imagine. But why was he so utterly devastated by what had happened? Did he—did Harry—come forward when Rob's father was in the bathtub? My God! It was Harry who killed him, mistaking his intentions! By drowning him, probably. When Rob saw what had happened, he ran away.

But this was only speculation of the worst kind. Maybe his father simply tried to get up, fell, and hit his head on the tub.

I had to find out the truth. And the only way to do that was to drag it out of Harry.

I cancelled my regular meeting with Giselle; I didn't want her to know anything she might inadvertently convey to prot, which might somehow tip off Harry. I looked over my schedule for the next three days. Booked solid. No time even for a quiet cup of coffee. There was nothing I could do but wait until Friday.

SESSION FORTY-THREE

THE *JEOPARDY* game took place in the lounge late Wednesday afternoon. The contestants, as voted on by the other patients, were "Albert Einstein," "Linus Pauling," and prot. There were no electronic signaling devices, no flashing scoreboards. Instead, hands were raised and Goldfarb was called upon to judge whose was first. Betty (who had managed to survive phase one of the root-canal procedure) kept the scores, and I was elected to blow the whistle when time was up for each half. The other patients and staff served as the audience.

Everything went very well at first, though Alex nervously brushed his hands through his wavy hair several times—I had never seen the real Alex Trebek do that. He had constructed his own category board and was, of course, quite familiar with the answers and questions. At the end of round one the scores were nearly even, much to the delight of the crowd. Every single answer had been properly questioned by one of the three contestants.

Then things began to fall apart. He got mixed up on an answer involving some arcane scientific term, and forgot where Patagonia was (he had some crib sheets, but couldn't seem to find what he needed in the rush and jumble). Albert and Linus tried to help, but prot just stood there with a silly grin on his face. Finally Alex stopped altogether and, despite lots of encouragement from the audience, threw down his notes and walked away, mumbling, "I don't want to be Alex Trebek. It's a lot harder than I thought."

"Do you think he's ready for Ward One?" Goldfarb whispered.

I countered, "Maybe we should wait until we're sure he doesn't want to be Mary Hart."

The new patients from the Big Institute arrived on Thursday, and a special orientation session was set up to acquaint them with their new home. This was done by pairing each of them with one of our long-term residents, who showed them around and introduced them to the rest of the inmates. However, the tours came to a halt in a big circle around prot, and there were the usual high expectations of what he could do for them once they were settled in, despite the limited time frame.

There were seven in all. One, a man suffering from DeClerambault's syndrome, was certain that Meg Ryan was in love with him. Another was constitutionally unable to tell the truth. (I was pretty sure what prot would do with him: suggest he run for public office.) Yet another thought himself the ugliest man in the world, a "toad," in his opinion.

The women in the group weren't much better off. There was a variant case of Cotan's syndrome (nothing exists), but in her case everything existed except her. To put it another way, she thought herself invisible to all of us and, consequently, felt no compulsion to dress after a shower, stole food from others' plates, etc. Another (my new responsibility) thought that real people were speaking to her from the television set. And there was a woman who simply could not get enough love (love, not sex). First thing she told her new doctor (Beamish) was that "No one ever called me 'J'aime.'" And finally, we had a new "Jesus Christ," but with a twist—she, too, was a woman, the first female Messiah to grace the institute in our long history. She had, of course, been a carpenter.

The "Magnificent Seven," Menninger called them. But all I could see was an enormous amount of frustrating work ahead. Like one of my previous charges, a postal carrier who went berserk because he could never finish the job ("No matter how many pieces I deliver they just keep coming!"), I could see a future with endless patients waiting to get in, like the people crowding around the front gate.

I had asked Jasmine Chakraborty to stand by in my office, which is adjacent to my examining room. (How he got his first name is a long story, and one of the reasons he left India.) Chak, too, had been making retirement noises lately, though he is only forty-eight. Or hinted, at least, that it was time "to make a new change," as he put it. I hoped he wasn't thinking of a move to the planet K-PAX.

Prot banged in and grabbed a huge handful of raisins, which he crammed into his mouth.

There was no more time to waste. "All right. I'd like to speak to Harry now. Harry?"

Prot seemed surprised, but stopped chewing and his feet began to shuffle around.

"Harry, this is Doctor Brewer. I'd like to speak with you for a minute."

Like Robert, Harry appeared to be hiding. But in his case, I could see him.

"Harry, c'mon out. If you don't, I'm coming in to get you."

Harry scowled, annoyed that he'd been found so easily. Apparently he didn't like raisins—he spat them back into his hand and dumped them onto the table next to the bowl.

"Harry, I'm mad as hell at you."

His feet stopped moving and his eyes opened wide. "I didn't do nothin'."

"Harry, what happened to Robin's father?"

"I didn't do it."

"Do what, Harry? What happened to Robin's dad?"

"He died."

"I know that. But how did he die? What happened to him?"

"I don't know. We ran out of the bathroom."

"Why? Why did you run out of the bathroom?"

"Rob was afraid."

"Of what? What was Robin afraid of, Harry?"

"He was afraid of his daddy."

"What was his daddy trying to do to him?"

"He swung at Robin."

"He tried to *hit* him?"

"Yes."

"Why?"

He seemed to shrink away from me. "I don't know!" It

occurred to me that perhaps he was lying about this to protect his alter ego. Or perhaps himself.

"Where did you run to?"

"We ran out into the woods. We was running as fast as we could. I tried to get Robin to slow down. He ran right straight into a tree. I tried to tell him to stop, but it was too late."

"What happened after that?"

Harry settled down a bit and started to chew on a fingernail. "I don't—I don't remember."

"What's the next thing you remember?"

"We were in bed and there were some people around."

"Who were they?"

"I don't know. They were strangers."

"Okay, Harry. I just want to ask you one more thing. Did you push Robin's father before you ran out? Or hit him with something? Anything like that?"

"No!"

"All right, Harry, just a couple more questions. Have you seen Robin lately?"

"Not for a long time."

"Do you know where he is?"

He shook his head.

"Okay, Harry, thank you. You've been very helpful. Now I'm going to ask you a big favor."

He looked puzzled.

"We need to take a little blood sample from you. It won't hurt much. You'll hardly feel it. Dr. Chakraborty works with me. He'll come in and do it, okay?"

He shifted around nervously. "What for?"

"We need to make sure it's all right. It's like a little checkup. You've been to the doctor before, haven't you?"

"No."

"Well, it'll only take a minute." I called Chak in.

Harry's mouth puckered up. "I don't want to. . . ."

The door opened. "Hi, Harry, how are you doing? I am Doctor Chakraborty. You may call me Doctor Jackrabbity if you want. I would like to take only a teensy-weensy bit of blood from your arm if you won't mind."

Harry started to squall. I thought: Here's a kid who may well have killed a grown man and he's afraid of a little needle. What a very strange thing is the human mind!

Chak tried to calm him by talking about his own five-year-old boy, who also hates to have blood taken. "Jag wants to be an astronaut, Harry. What do you want to be?"

Harry wasn't interested in discussing it. He was crying his eyes out.

"Okay, Gene, I'm finished."

"Harry? It's all over. Thank you for coming in. You may go now."

The crying ceased immediately. Harry was out of here.

Before prot could return I called out, "Paul? This is Dr. Brewer. May I speak to you for a moment?"

Paul yawned. "That was a pretty dirty trick you pulled on old Harry, there. You didn't tell him you were going to suck blood out of him." He grabbed the pile of chewed-up raisins and popped them back into his mouth. "If you had, he never would have showed up."

"Paul, this is Dr. Chakraborty. He'd like to take a little from you, too."

"Sure. Why not?" He held out his arm.

"Other arm, please," Chak said.

While "Dr. Jackrabbity" was preparing a fresh needle and

syringe, I asked Paul if he knew anything about the death of Rob's father. "Not a thing," he said. "I wasn't around then."

"I know. But I thought you might have heard something. From Rob or Harry—someone."

"Nope."

"Finished."

"Thanks, Chak."

"There is no problem," he said as he hurried out with the precious blood samples.

"Seen Rob anywhere around today?" I asked Paul.

He began to tap a foot nervously. "Nope."

"Do you know where he is? How we might find him?"

"No idea."

"Well, where did he go in the past when prot showed up?"

He shrugged. "I never paid much attention. When prot came, my chances of gettin' laid were nil or less."

"Speaking of that, I need to ask you a very important question, and I would appreciate a truthful answer."

He looked pained, but didn't protest his honesty.

"Paul, I know you come out whenever Rob has a sexual encounter. What I want to know is whether you ever pretended to be Robert at other times. Specifically, in this room."

His face actually turned red, and he said, sheepishly, "Once in a while."

"When, for example?"

"When you talked about his sex life. He doesn't even like to *think* about it, you know."

"No other times?"

"Hardly ever."

"And Rob was really Rob in his other dealings with Giselle?"

"I really don't care about the rest of his life, doc."

"Okay, Paul. You may go."

"What—already?"

"Just wanted to take a blood sample. Thanks. Bye-bye."

"You got some damn good-looking nurses around here, you know that? I'd sure like to—"

"Good-bye, Paul. Thanks for stopping by. I'll call you again if I need you."

He stared at me glumly, but finally went back to wherever he hung out when he wasn't needed.

Prot reappeared and went again for the bowl of raisins. "Any luck, doctor b?"

"Another strikeout."

"Ah, those handy sports terms." Bits of the dried fruit flew from his mouth. "Y'all seem to think life is just one big ball game."

"Is that so bad?"

"Even your so-called scientists spend most of their time playing games when the answers are right there staring them in the face."

I brushed a bit of raisin off my knee. "What answers?"

"Well, for example, whether the UNIVERSE is going to collapse again or expand forever."

"According to my son-in-law, some astronomers think it's going to be an endless expansion."

"So what? You haven't got all the evidence yet. Why do you humans tend to jump to conclusions before all the facts are in?"

"I think everyone realizes this is mostly speculation," I replied weakly. "Anyway, why don't you give us some hints if you already have all the answers?"

"Okay, since you can't destroy anyone with it, though you'd probably like to, I'll give you a hint. The 'missing mass' is right there in Einstein's equations. You just haven't put two and two together yet."

"Thanks. I'll pass that on."

He tipped up the bowl and took in the last raisin. "Well, if there's nothing else . . ."

"There *is* one thing. Have you had a chance to talk with any of the new patients?"

"Sure."

"What do you think?"

"About what?"

"Dammit, prot, about the patients!"

"Sorry, doctor. I've decided to retire from psychoanalysis. They're your responsibility from now on."

"Wonderful."

"Don't underestimate yourselves. You can do it. You've just got to get rid of a lot of the false assumptions you seem to cherish. Believe me, it's as simple as that." He stood and stretched. "Well, I've got things to do. *Au revoir.*"

"But our time isn't—"

After the door slammed I thought: Another session wasted. I didn't even press him on the question of how Rob's (or his own) father died. On second thought, it wasn't a total bust. I was convinced that Rob, in the guise of Harry, at least, didn't kill his father. But if he had drowned accidentally, how did it happen? Maybe I was trying to make too much of the situation. Perhaps prot was wrong and he *did* die of natural causes. In either case, why would Rob feel so incredibly guilty about it? What the hell was it he wanted and very much needed to "get off his chest," but could not?

It was time to play the trump card. To get his "dad" in here to confront Rob, to get the truth out of him before it was too late.

That evening I called Steve and told him about prot's advice to the world's astronomers. To my surprise, he seemed quite excited about this. "Einstein's equations? You mean general relativity?" There was a long pause and I thought for a minute he had gone. "Only problem," he went on, "is how does that help us to find the missin' mass?" Another pause. "Unless he's sayin' it has somethin' to do with acceleration and gravity. . . ." I heard panting. "Mah God!" he shrieked. "That's it!"

"Steve? Steve?"

I called back a few seconds later but the line was busy.

On Saturday night, while Karen and I were decorating the tree (less than two weeks to Christmas and I hadn't done any shopping yet), a middle-aged man came to the door. He was unshaven, his eyes bloodshot, but his clothes were clean, if threadbare and patched. I thought he was looking for work or a handout, though he didn't seem to be drunk or schizophrenic, as many homeless people are. "Got a match?" he squeaked in a hoarse, high-pitched voice. I didn't, but I hesitated to let him in. His face, however, was drawn, and he seemed to be in pain. His breath was raspy. I told him to wait and I would see if I could find one.

As I turned toward the living room I heard him say, "Aren't you going to let me in?" The voice had dropped an octave and had become much stronger. "Remember the Robert Frost poem you read to us when we were kids? Home is where—"

"Fred!"

He grinned. "Well, were you convinced?"

"I certainly was! That's exactly how I imagined Robert's father would be like!"

"Let's hope that's the way Robert remembers him!" He took off his coat and headed for the living room. "If I know you guys, you're decorating the Christmas tree tonight."

SESSION FORTY-FOUR

N O STAFF meeting on the fifteenth; this was the day of the outing to the Met Museum, one of four seasonal "getaways" we provide for all the patients who can, and want to, go. As luck would have it, I decided not to take part, opting instead to speak to the building contractor and get some other nagging work done.

It was a sunny day, and nearly all the patients in Wards One and Two (with a smattering of Threes) gathered on the front lawn, some of them toting a cat. Prot, of course, took this opportunity to address the crowd outside the gate, reiterating his regret that he could take none of them with him to K-PAX, reminding them that there wasn't much time left to change things here (on Earth), and all the rest. None of the visitors seemed to want to leave, however, until he departed for the museum.

While waiting for the bus to arrive, prot, like some two-legged sheepdog, herded everyone tightly together in the center of the front lawn. Without a word he produced a small flashlight, placed it on his shoulder, aimed it at a little mirror he pulled out from somewhere, and suddenly (according to both the hospital staff and eyewitnesses outside the gate) everyone disappeared.

"It was unbelievable," Betty told me later (they came back on the bus). "One minute we were standing on the lawn, the next we were on the steps of the Met. But there wasn't any sensation of movement at all, or of time passing. In fact, nobody felt a thing."

I should point out here that the integrity of Betty McAllister is beyond reproach. Moreover, Drs Beamish and Chang breathlessly confirmed everything she told me. Not having witnessed the event myself, however, I was still dubious, to put it mildly. "Are you sure you weren't the victim of some sort of hypnotic trick?" I asked her.

"I thought of that, too. But how do you explain the accounts of all the people outside the fence who saw us disappear?"

"Maybe they were fooled, too."

"What about the surveillance cameras? Did you see the tapes?"

"I saw them."

"Well? Can't you admit, finally, that he's who he says he is?"

"Maybe and maybe not," I said, thoroughly confused. "It still could be some kind of trick."

I had known Betty for twenty-five years, and we had always gotten along extremely well. But what she said next stung me to the quick. "Gene," she exclaimed, "you're blind as a bat!"

"You could be right about that. But my responsibility is

still to my patient, Robert Porter. What do you suggest I do about *him*?"

Unfortunately, she, like prot and everyone else, had no easy answer for that.

I left Fred in my office with Giselle and stepped into the examining room. Two weeks left, and I was so damn tired I didn't know whether I could keep up with prot for even that long. In fact, when he came in he caught me dozing. I awoke with a jolt and stared blankly at him, wondering who he was. "Did you really take forty people to the Met yesterday?" I demanded when I realized where we were.

He took a huge bite out of a pineapple and nodded matter-of-factly.

"Then why did you ride the bus back?"

"Thought I'd take one last look at the city."

"I see. And what did you think of it?"

"I thought: At the rate you're going, the whole EARTH will look like this some day."

"Is that such a bad thing?"

"It is if you're a giraffe."

We had already wasted enough time. "All right. Let's get down to business."

He wagged his head and blurted out a chuckle.

"Giselle got us a copy of the death certificate. You were right—it's somewhat vague on the cause of death. Would you like to elaborate on that?"

"Not particularly."

"Okay, damn it, would you please tell me what you know, even if you wouldn't like to?"

"He fell and hit his head."

"Was he pushed, or was it an accident?"

Prot shrugged. "How should I know?"

"You won't help me at all on this?"

"I *am* helping you. You just don't realize it yet."

"All right, fine. I'd like to speak to Robert now."

"No hypnotic tricks?"

"I don't think we're going to need that anymore."

He swallowed the last chunk of pineapple, murmured, "He's all yours," and his head sank to his chest.

"Rob?"

Of course there was no response.

"Rob, I have a surprise for you today. How would you like to see your father again?"

His head jerked, as if it had been tapped with a sledge-hammer. But he said nothing.

"He's waiting outside, Rob."

I heard him swallow, as though he were choking back a sob.

"Shall I ask him to come in?"

He made a few more guttural noises.

"Well, if you don't want to see him, I'll just ask him to go." I stood up and moved toward the door. There was a definite strangled whine. "Maybe he can come back in a week or two." I added, reaching for the knob.

"Noooooooooooo!" he gurgled. "Please! I want to see my daddy!"

I motioned for Fred to come in. He went straight to my patient and put a hand on his shoulder. "Hi, Robbie," he rasped. "I've missed you."

Rob fell to his knees, weeping much like Linus had earlier.

He thrust his arms around Fred's legs and repeated, over and over again, "I'm sorry, Daddy. I'm so sorry. Oh, God, I'm so sorry. . . ."

I began to gurgle a little myself. It was exactly what I had been waiting to hear. What I didn't expect, however, was what happened next. Robert gasped, rolled over, and passed out.

While I ran to examine him, Fred, taken aback, apologized for what had happened. "I'm sorry, Dad. I didn't mean to—"

"Not your fault, Freddy. You were perfect." Rob, however, had gone back to his familiar catatonic state. He had finally unloaded the thing he had wanted to get off his chest. Now it was simply a matter of pulling him out of the catatonia. Unfortunately, that could take years.

Only then did it occur to me that this was exactly the state Rob had been left in seven years ago. Had prot gone somewhere else? "Prot? Prot?"

He sat up. "How did I get down on the floor, coach? Howdy, Fred."

"You left us for a while."

"I didn't get very far, did I?"

"I'd say it was a giant step."

"But of course you want *two* giant steps."

"I'll settle for your delaying your trip to K-PAX for another five years."

"Sorry."

"In that case, that's all for today. And prot?"

"Narr?"

"Please don't take any more of the patients or staff from the hospital grounds without permission, okay?"

He held up three fingers, as if giving the Boy Scout oath,

and said, solemnly, "I hereby promise not to take any of the patients or staff from the hospital grounds. Until the thirty-first of December, of course." He saluted and left.

After he had gone Fred confided, "I used to think you just sat around gabbing all day, Dad. I had no idea what you really did. Now I see it's a lot of work and a big responsibility. And I think you're probably very good at your job."

All I could think of in reply was, "Your work isn't nearly as easy as I thought either, son."

He hugged me. "I've always wanted to hear you say that." Neither of us wanted to let go. Of each other, of moments like this, of sweet life.

We finally went to my inner office, where Giselle was waiting. Freddy asked her if he might be able to talk to prot that morning (I had told him she was acting as prot's "Chief of Staff"). She said she thought that could be arranged. I wondered whether something was bothering him that he wanted to discuss with our "alien" friend, but I didn't want to bring up personal or family matters in front of Giselle. She may have been like a daughter to me, but she had only seen Fred once or twice.

Inasmuch as he had been instrumental in getting through to Rob, on the other hand, it seemed perfectly reasonable to report to her, with Fred present, on the progress we had made that morning.

"Rob was there?" she exclaimed. "He spoke to you?"

"Of course he was there!" I exclaimed in return. "Don't you understand that wherever prot is, Rob is there, too?"

"Not necessarily," Fred interposed.

I was wondering whether I should have left him outside. "Why do you say that?"

"Well, his father was there a little while ago, but his father wasn't there."

"But MPD is a far different thing from playacting, Fred."

"Maybe. But how do you know it wasn't just prot pretending to be Rob? Or maybe it's been Rob all along pretending to be prot. Or someone else altogether pretending to be all of them. For that matter, how do you know that multiple personality disorder isn't really just a matter of playacting?"

My son, the shrink. I didn't have time to give him a lecture on the principles of psychiatry, but I did point out that the various personalities originating from a single individual exhibit a number of differences in physical characteristics.

"Anybody ever do any tests like that with actors playing different roles?" he wondered.

Unfortunately, we didn't have an opportunity to pursue the matter. Fred had an audition coming up, and Giselle escorted him to Ward Two and his "consultation" with prot. Nor had I had the chance to tell her that her husband had slipped into a state of catatonia once again.

I sat there trying to make sense of what had happened. But I couldn't get Fred's questions out of my mind. It did, in fact, seem that Paul had been impersonating Rob at least part of the time in 1995. Did he come out that morning, pretending to be Robert, to apologize to his father for him? Was it possible he could have been playing the role of Harry as well? Or, for that matter, prot? Or was I making too much of all this? Wasn't it more likely that what had transpired in my examining room was exactly what it seemed to be: The grief and guilt underlying Rob's illness was born of something he had done to his father?

Was it, in fact, a mercy killing, rather than an assisted suicide, an attempt to end his father's suffering, something that neither Harry nor Paul participated in?

Maybe it was time to admit that this case was too much for me. To admit that I might never find out what was behind Robert Porter's problems. To call in someone else. But the only person who seemed to be able to help with such a tangled case was prot himself, whoever he was.

Session Forty-five

A FTER THE alleged flight to the Met, many of the staff, as well as virtually all of the patients, of course, were now firmly convinced that prot was who he said he was. Not long after that unbelievable journey I got a call from the research ophthalmologist who had wanted to examine prot's visual capabilities in 1995 (after learning that he was able to see ultraviolet light, much as certain insects and a few other earthly creatures can do).

"You'll have to talk to Giselle Griffin about that."

"I already did. She told me to call you."

"All I can do is ask him."

Since it would have been difficult to truck all of the necessary equipment up to MPI, I sent prot, who was perfectly willing to cooperate in this venture—perhaps he had finalized his list of fellow travelers—to Dr. Sternik's office and laboratory at NYU, along with a security officer. They left on Wednesday morning and didn't return until late afternoon.

Sternik called me at six o'clock, just as I was packing my briefcase to leave. When I had talked to him earlier his voice was steady, confident. Now he spoke uncertainly in quavery tones, obviously shaken. He confirmed that prot could see light down to around 400 Å and added, "I've examined every part of his eyes and they are quite normal in all other respects. Unusually healthy eyes, in fact. Except for his retinas. Besides the usual rods and cones, there seem to be little hexagonal crystals scattered around the fovea. Whether they have anything to do with his ultraviolet vision or not, I haven't a clue. But I've never seen anything like it. . . ."

I waited for him to go on. There wasn't much I could offer, anyway.

"I was wondering," he said finally, "whether prot would be willing to donate one of his eyes to us."

"Well, I don't—"

"In the event of his death, of course. I think we might learn some very interesting things from those retinas."

I promised him I would speak to prot about it. "But he's leaving us on the thirty-first."

"Leaving? Where's he going?"

"Says he's going back to the planet he came from."

Without a moment's hesitation he cried out, "I'll give him a hundred thousand dollars for an eye!"

I promised to pass on the offer, but advised him not to hold his breath.

The next day I was swamped with patients, meetings (one in mid-town), and my regular lecture at Columbia, the last of the semester, during which I had to cram in all the material

I hadn't gotten to earlier. On top of everything else I had suffered through another restless night, with thoughts of recent events racing around in my head at tachyon speed. But all of them kept circling round and round the central question: Who was prot? Suppose he was an alien from halfway across the galaxy, or Santa Claus, or the tooth fairy, or God Himself. How would this help my patient, Robert Porter? I pondered the alternative—that he was merely an alter ego, a human being from Guelph, Montana. Whatever he was, Robert remained catatonic. When I finally got up I felt a bit more achy than usual and a little lightheaded, and I wondered whether I was coming down with something. It couldn't be the flu, I told myself; I had been vaccinated in October along with the rest of the staff.

Somehow I got through the morning (though I fell asleep during a session with one of my patients, the first time I had ever done so). I was tempted to cancel the lecture, but how could I? It was the last one, and I still had enough material for three more classes.

But the students had heard about the lightning-quick trip to the museum, and already knew about the results of prot's retinal exam. Bleary-eyed, I threw my notebook on the desk, gave them a huge reading assignment, assured them that everything I hadn't discussed in class would be on the final exam, and told them exactly where the case of Robert Porter stood. What the hell, I rationalized, maybe they could come up with something I hadn't.

The discussion was led, of course, by "Doctor Sacks," who declared: "It's as plain as the nose on your face. The father asked his son to help him commit suicide. It probably took many discussions out on the lawn at night, in the guise of watching the stars, but finally, as his dad got worse and worse, the boy became convinced. Now imagine his dilemma—here he was, six years old, and his beloved father was in enormous pain. Wouldn't you want to help him end the misery? At the same time he knew it was wrong to kill his father. He was caught between a rock and a hard place. One night his father said he couldn't stand it any longer. He begged Rob to help him do it. Maybe the boy held him down in the tub, or tied him down so he couldn't get out, something like that. Of course when it was all over and he realized what he had done, he ran out of the bathroom and kept on running, trying to get away from it all. But no matter how far or how fast he ran, he couldn't get away from himself. Not in a million years. It would be enough to drive anyone crazy!"

"And how does prot fit into all this?"

"He called out for help. Prot was the only one who heard him."

"You think he came from K-PAX to help someone he didn't even know?"

"He's here, ain't he?"

I dismissed the class early and went home.

The next day I had a low-grade fever, pain in every joint. I've always thought that people who are sick should stay home and not spread their illness to everyone they might come into contact with. But there was no choice—I *had* to keep my appointment with prot. So, feeling like a Typhoid Mary, I forced myself to get up and go to the hospital.

I shuffled in a few minutes late for our session. He was

already in his usual place, gorging on tangerines. "Prot, I'd like to talk to you."

"Talk away."

"But first I'd like to speak to Rob."

He gawked around. "Where is he?"

"Never mind that for now. Please—just sit back and relax."

He sighed and rolled his UV-sensitive eyes, but his head finally drooped down.

"Rob?"

No response.

"Rob, I want to apologize to you for what I said a couple of sessions ago. I accused your father of attacking you in the bathroom. Now I think it was something else. It may have been an accident. He may have fallen and hit his head. But I don't think you'd feel all this guilt if that were the case."

I waited a minute to let this sink in. If he agreed, he didn't acknowledge it.

"Rob, did your father ask you to help him kill himself? I think he did, and you finally agreed. But you were over-whelmed with guilt about this, weren't you, Rob? Isn't that why you ran out of the bathroom when it was over?"

There was no indication that he had even heard me.

"Okay. Thank you, Rob. You may go. Prot?"

His head came up.

"All right. I'm putting the white dot back on the wall. Go ahead and hypnotize yourself whenever you're ready."

When I turned around, he was already "out."

"Good. Now I'd like to speak to Robert again. Rob? C'mon out, Rob—I know you're there." When nothing happened I repeated almost verbatim the speech I had given a few minutes earlier, ending with the suggestion that he had been talked

233

into helping his father commit suicide. "You had no choice, Rob. Under the circumstances, I would probably have done the same thing. Almost anybody would have."

Again there wasn't the slightest acknowledgment.

At this point I decided there was nothing to lose by playing the only card left in the deck. "But he didn't just ask you to help him die, did he, Rob? In fact, he *made* you do it, didn't he? He threatened to tell your mother about Uncle Dave, didn't he? And if he did that, your Uncle Dave would kill you, isn't that right?"

The only response was a kind of deep sigh, more like a snore.

"That wasn't a very nice thing your father did to you, was it, Rob? In fact, you realized he was no better than your uncle. You knew he would take advantage of you at every opportunity. You realized then that your father wasn't a god, as you had thought. In fact, he was just the opposite. *Your father was a piece of shit, wasn't he, Rob?*"

He made another noise, but I didn't wait for more.

"You hated him, didn't you, Rob? You hated him with all the passion in your young soul, with all the frustration and disgust you felt for Uncle Dave. You took your frustration and hopelessness out on your father, didn't you? You grabbed a baseball bat or something, and when he was in the bathtub and couldn't get away from you, you let him have it, isn't that right? You killed him, didn't you? You brought that club down on his head and watched him sink into the water, isn't that what happened? Isn't it, Rob? *ISN'T IT?*"

His head came up and his eyes, like those of some animal in the dark, flashed at me. "You fucking asshole!" he snarled. "You dirty, rotten bastard! You motherfucking son-of-a-bitch! You're the dumbest, lousiest, shittiest turd in the universe! *I loved my father. Can't you understand that? He was the most wonderful man in the world. That's why I . . ."*

"What, Rob? What did you do to your father?"

But he had broken down sobbing. At last, at last, at long last, I thought: This is what I've been waiting for. "All right, Rob, I understand. Take your time. When you're—"

"That's why I tried to do to Daddy what Uncle Dave wanted me to do with him!" He broke down completely. "Oh, God, I can't stand it!"

With all the strength I could muster I grabbed his shoulders and shook them. "Rob, stay with me for just a minute longer! Are you saying you tried to—"

Still sobbing, he stuttered, "That's when he took a swing at me. And then he tried to get up. But he slipped and fell and banged his head on the back of the tub. He was dead, I knew it. So I ran away. Oh, Daddy, I'm so sorry. Please, please forgive me! I was only trying to make you feel better. . . ." That was the last word he said before his voice trailed off into a long, diminishing wail.

I waited a few minutes, vainly hoping he would get hold of himself, but there wasn't a movement or a sound. I sank down in my chair. "Thank you, Rob," I whispered. "Thank you for trusting me, my friend. The worst of it is over. Now you can rest. You can finally rest. . . . Prot?"

"Hiya, doc. What next?"

"Please unhypnotize— Thank you."

"What for?"

"For all your help."

"You're welcome, doc." He seemed puzzled. "You said you

wanted to talk to me after you spoke with Robert. Was that what you wanted to tell me?"

"Not exactly. I was going to ask you what you know about retrieving someone from the catatonic state. But now I don't think that will be necessary. I think he's going to be okay."

"He told you that?"

"Not in so many words."

"Well, I'll hold his seat open a little while longer, just in case he's changed his mind. You know how these human beings are." He turned briskly and hurried out the door.

I sat for a long time after he had gone, just staring after him. How lucky I had been to get into medicine, and then psychiatry. How I wish I could thank my father for pushing me into it!

That state of euphoria lasted about ten seconds. Then I remembered we still had a very long way to go to lead Robert out of the maze. And, despite everything we had accomplished, it might never happen. Totally exhausted, I fell asleep in my chair. It was another hour before Betty found me. I had missed an assignment committee meeting in which two more of our patients were judged to be ready for Ward One.

I slept almost the whole weekend, and still felt weak on Monday. Nonetheless I made it to the hospital in time for the regular staff meeting.

The hot topic for discussion this time was Frankie. It appeared that over the last few days she had suddenly rallied, lost all her bitterness toward the human race and become almost cheerful. Everyone looked at me; she was, after all, my patient, and had been for more than two years. I shrugged feebly, murmured something about a virus.

"Sounds like prot's work," Thorstein observed. "I wonder how he did it."

Everyone looked at me again. "I'll ask him," was all I could come up with. The refrain was becoming all too familiar.

But I ran into Frankie first. She was in the exercise room doing calisthenics, something I had never seen her engage in, nor any other kind of game or exercise. "How are you feeling?" I asked her inanely.

"Wonderful. Fine fucking day, isn't it?" She continued the rhythmic, mesmerizing jumping jacks, the blobs of fat slightly out of sync with the rest of her body. One of the cats, who normally would have nothing to do with her, watched her bounce up and down like a ping-pong ball.

"Yes, it is. So—have you been talking to prot?"

"Once or twice."

"Did he tell you anything that might have cheered you up at all?"

Perspiring and breathing heavily, she switched to a series of squat thrusts. "Now that you mention it, he did." She farted loudly.

The "two Al's" happened to come by. "I'd recognize one of your glaciermelters anywhere," Albert snorted. (This wasn't such a silly statement, actually. Recent studies have shown that the feces of the mentally ill contain chemicals related to the nature of their illnesses. Shit happens, and it is telling.)

"Could you tell me what it was he said to you, Frankie? Did he give you a 'task' or something?"

"That's affirmative," she puffed.

"What was it? To start exercising?"

"Egg-zack-a-tickly. He told me to get in shape for a very goddamned long journey."

I thought: Oh, shit! "Did he say what journey you needed to prepare for?"

She merely looked up toward the sky with a very prot-like grin.

"You want to consider a transfer to Ward One?"

"No, thanks," she grunted. "Not worth the trouble."

SESSION FORTY-SIX

"How's the virus?" prot asked me when he came in. I started to say I was feeling better, but quickly realized he might be inquiring about the well-being of the bugs themselves. He downed half-a-dozen pomegranates in about three minutes. After he had finished and settled into his chair, I asked whether he was, in fact, going to take Frankie with him to K-PAX.

"She's not very happy here, wouldn't you say, gino?"

"Seemed to be doing all right when I saw her yesterday."

"That's because she knows she'll be getting out of here soon."

"To K-PAX."

"Yep. Where none of the terrible things that befell her on EARTH can happen to her."

"Because there are none of us lowly human beings there, you mean."

"You said it, I didn't."

"But Frankie is human! So is Bess!"

"No they aren't! That's why you locked them up here in your jail!"

"They aren't *Homo sapiens*?"

"Of course they are. But being 'human,' my dear sir, is a state of mind. And a nasty one at that."

"All right. Who else is on your list?"

"Only ninety-nine other beings, unfortunately."

"All right, Mr. Spock. I'd like to speak with Robert now."

"Very well, captain." His head drooped down slightly. It was a familiar sight.

"Rob? Can we talk?"

He declined the offer.

I was on thin ice again, but I remembered one of our former director Klaus Villers' maxims: Extraordinary cases require extraordinary measures. "Rob, what do you think of going to K-PAX with prot? Everything would be different there. You could forget the past, get a fresh start. Does that idea appeal to you?"

There was no sign it did.

"I'll tell you what. Just nod if you'd like to get away from all this. Do you want to go to K-PAX, Rob?"

I watched him closely for any sign of movement. It was barely possible even to tell whether he was breathing.

"Rob, there's something you may not know. On K-PAX you would be able to see your father again any time you want. Did you know that?"

I thought he jerked his head a little, though it might have been wishful thinking on my part.

"That's right, Rob, they have a wonderful device there, a computer with all-sense capability. You can roam the fields of

240

your boyhood, wrestle the Hulk, visit with your father before he was injured in the slaughterhouse, play chess or watch the stars with him, whatever you'd like to do. Sound good?"

Was it a hint of a smile I saw, or only my imagination?

"You could talk to your father, tell him how sorry you are, and life would go on as if nothing had happened. Would you like that, Rob? Think about it!"

I literally felt my heart jump as his head slowly began to rise. Slowly, slowly, slowly. Finally, he murmured, "Would Giselle and our son get to go, too? I'd like Dad to meet them."

I choked back a sob. "That's up to prot, Rob. Want to speak to him about it?"

He nodded once before his head fell back to his chest. Almost immediately he looked up again. "Was Robert here?"

"You just missed him."

"I thought I felt some pretty strong vibes."

"He was right here, prot. But only for a minute or two. See if you can find him, will you? He can't have gone far." My eyes were very tired, and I closed them for a moment. The next thing I knew I was alone; both prot and Robert were gone.

Giselle, of course, was elated that Rob might be going to K-PAX. Before I could tell her the rationale for my promise to him, she exclaimed, "I've got so much to do!"

"Wait!"

She whirled around. "Yes?"

"What will you do if Rob changes his mind again?"

"I haven't got time for mind games, Dr. B. I've got to find prot. See you later!"

I wondered, sadly, what would happen when prot "departed" and left all three of them behind. Would I have the whole Porter family as patients? I went home to try to recover from the lingering effects of the virus and to discuss retirement plans with my wife.

It finally turned colder on Christmas Eve, and seemed more like winter. Nonetheless, the crowd outside the front gate was still in an upbeat mood, drinking hot beverages obtained from a vendor and singing songs of the season. Someone had even put up a Christmas tree, which had been decorated with stars of all sizes and shapes. I could also see a menorah or two, candles lit. Not Rockefeller Center, but beautiful nonetheless.

Nothing much was going on inside the walls. It was a day of parties in all the wards, the first in Ward Four, and we worked our way down from there. I still didn't feel well enough to play Santa Claus, and turned that duty over to prot, who delighted in belting out "Ho, ho, ho's" at every turn. There was a gift for each of the residents, and cake and punch. The psychopaths were released from their cells one or two at a time. Perhaps it was only the spirit of the season, but they all seemed in complete control, not an evil thought among them. Even Charlotte, in her orange shackles, seemed cheerful and composed. Of course she has always gotten along well with men, right up to the time she bites off some part of their anatomy.

Ward Three was a bit more relaxed, there being little danger to the staff except for the odd pie in the face or the rare occasion when one of the sexual deviates occasionally pinched a nurse.

I found Jerry working on a perfect replica of the Statue of Liberty, right down to the patina of green oxides and the little silvery sun reflector in her torch. "Some cake or cookies, Jerry? They're your favorite—chocolate chip!"

"Chocolate chip, chocolate chip, chocolate chip," he mumbled, apparently without comprehension. But he grabbed the one I offered and whisked it into his mouth without missing a beat. I watched him work for a while, wondering, as I did so, how prot had managed to get through to him two years earlier and why the rest of us couldn't. Maybe he was right – if we could learn to really feel what they feel . . . But I was too old to start over. I only hoped my son Will and "Oliver" and the rest of their generation would have more success than I, that psychiatry would soon be making the kinds of miraculous strides being revealed almost daily in other fields of medicine. And I thought: What a wonderful time to be born!

The Ward Two party was combined with Ward One's. I'd never seen the patients in such a happy state. Especially the "Magnificent Seven," who seemed to be an optimistic bunch, despite their various problems. I wondered whether they were anticipating visits to "Dr. prot" and expecting to move down to One soon, as had Albert and Alice, who were perfectly all right as long as they stayed together. Indeed, having little choice, apparently, they were planning to be married as soon as they were discharged.

Alex had brought some work to the party. He was one of those who had been transferred to One, having announced he wanted to be a librarian. What could be more sane? He was reading a book called *Computers for Nitwits*. When I asked him about it he explained that everything was on computers these days. "Why, I wouldn't be surprised if books and magazines became obsolete altogether!" I could only hope he was wrong about that. Karen and I had planned to spend a significant part of our retirement devouring all the books we had never found time to read.

The changes in Linus and Ophelia were tremendous. Linus was the happiest guy at the party—somewhere he had found a cowboy hat and was practicing his rope twirling—and Ophelia the loudest. In fact, she wanted to order everyone around, trying to make up for lost time, I suppose. Well, I thought, not all sane people are angels.

I found prot surrounded by several of the other patients, and the usual dozen cats. I was surprised when he asked to speak with me. Everyone else pretended to be annoyed, but they knew he wouldn't be far away. Not, at least, until the thirty-first.

When we were ensconced in a corner he said, "Robert sends you his apologies."

"For what?"

"He won't be seeing you again."

"You spotted him?"

"Yep."

"But we have two more sessions!"

"He has nothing more to tell you before he goes."

All I could think of was: God Almighty, what have I done? "What about Giselle and little Gene?"

"We'll work something out."

"Still scheduled for December thirty-first?"

"Right after breakfast."

"Can't you—"

"No way, José."

"In that case," I sighed, "I wonder whether you'd like to

spend Christmas with Karen and me. Abby and Steve and the kids will be there too, and maybe Fred."

"Why, shore, if there aren't any dead birds on the table (I had told him about the soy turkey on Thanksgiving).

"They all want to say good-bye."

"Where they going?"

It rained on Christmas. Betty and her husband brought prot, but that was the last they saw of him that day. Steve, who had been appointed acting chair of the astronomy department now that Flynn was combing the world for supplies of spider excrement, cornered him most of the time. I didn't mind. After toying with the idea of trying to call forth Robert, I decided against it. Seeing all the food and gifts and decorations might have brought back childhood memories and made things even worse. This would be a non-session. Only Will, who was spending the holiday with Dawn's family in Cleveland, was missing. And, of course, Jenny out in California. But both called to wish us a Merry Christmas and it was almost as if we were all together again.

Steve wanted to know everything prot had to tell him about the moment before the Big Bang, whether there was really a theory of everything, how soon the universe would stop expanding and begin to contract, what would happen at the time of the Big Crunch, and so on. Above all, however, he wanted prot to be the first to know that his newly programmed computer confirmed his hypothesis that if the expansion of the universe were accelerating, a new cosmological constant would slow it back down again.

Prot yawned. "Yes, I know."

"One more thing: Hawking has said that even though nothing can escape from black holes, they can still leak radiation. True or false?"

"False!"

"They don't?"

"No—they can leak *everything*! Otherwise how do you explain the BIG BANG, which started out as the BLACKEST HOLE of all time?"

"How can I thank you for putting me on to all this?"

"Tell your fellow humans to stay away from the STARS until they learn that all the other beings in the UNIVERSE aren't there for their benefit."

Later, when we had gathered around the table, he remarked, "You humans are at your best this time of year, when you begin to notice there are other people around besides yourselves. Why not share this generosity of spirit with the other beings on your PLANET, just for this one day?" He finished his glüg (Karen is of Scandinavian origin) and asked for more.

Abby, at least, had long been convinced. This time it was a yam duck. And Karen had prepared his usual enormous fruit salad. Prot gobbled it all down, then sat back and patted his bulging stomach. "I'm going to have to go on a diet when I get back," he sighed. I thought: How very human!

The subject turned to our plans for the upcoming year, beginning with the New Year's Eve party Karen was planning for all our friends. Someone brought up the subject of the big celebration two years hence.

"One of the saddest things about your beings," prot informed us, "is that you're all looking forward to a new millennium, when things will be better than they are now. But you're all going to wake up in the next century and everything will be just like it was before. Except for one thing, of course," he added, almost as an afterthought. "It will be your last."

But Rain wasn't convinced. "Prot, what's the first thing we have to do in order to survive the next century?"

"Everything."

"Everything?"

"It's all interrelated. For example, you can't reduce your numbers until you eliminate your religious beliefs. And you can't do that as long as there is an abundance of ignorance and a dearth of education. But you can't change that as long as people with the most money use it to maintain the status quo. And if you maintain the status quo, your environment will soon collapse. But you can't protect the environment from collapse until you reduce your numbers—shall I go on?"

"Let's open the presents first!" shouted Star, to everyone's relief.

There were the usual gifts—ties, shaving lotion, computer games for the kids, a squeaky toy for Oxie, dried fruit for prot. But there were also presents under the tree *from* him. He handed one of them to me. "You first."

Hoping not to find any unwanted surprises, I carefully opened the little box. Inside was a smaller one. And inside that an even smaller one. And inside that there was one so tiny I was sure I would never be able to get it open. I didn't know whether to laugh or cry. The others opened their gifts and, without a word being spoken, everyone carefully separated his or her pea-sized box from the rest.

"Let's sprinkle them on the tree," Star suggested, and we all did so.

Prot lifted his glass and wished us all a Merry Christmas.

"And a happy retirement to all the fogeys present. May they live a thousand years!" Glasses clinked like so many bells.

Afterward, while Steve was having his last shot at prot, I cornered Fred to report on Robert's progress. "He's through the worst of it," I assured him. "Now I think he can accept what happened to him and go on to the next stage—grief. Fortunately, given enough time, we can do something about that."

He nodded, but seemed distracted by something. It appeared that this was the moment he had chosen to tell me what had been bothering him recently. Or perhaps longer. If he didn't want to be an actor anymore (and I understood how difficult the profession was), what then? Was it possible he had decided he wanted to be a doctor, like me? Would there be another psychiatrist in the family? I prodded him a little. "Were you able to talk to prot the other day?"

"Yes. He helped me to decide."

"Decide what?"

"To tell you something I've been wanting to tell you for a long time."

I didn't like the sound of that. "I'm listening, son."

"Dad," he blurted out, "I don't want the house, and I don't want to get married."

"You mean—"

"No, I'm not gay. In fact, I've got more women than I can handle."

"I thought it was the ballerina."

"Actually, it's two ballerinas and a flight attendant and an assistant producer. At the moment."

"Sounds like you need help, Fred."

"No, thanks, Dad. I'm having way too much fun. It's the

house I wanted to talk to you about, mostly. I know you were thinking of passing it on, and I know how much it means to you to keep it in the family. But it's not right for me. And neither is the suburban life."

"Why now, Freddy? Why are you telling me now?"

"I think it was what happened in your examining room. I didn't want to be sorry later on, when it might be too late, for not sharing these things with you."

That I could understand.

"Does this mean you don't want to be a psychiatrist?"

"Why in the world would I want to be a psychiatrist? I love acting. In fact, I was going to tell you that I just got promoted to the Broadway production of *Les Mis*!"

It was my turn to hug *him*. "That's great news, Freddy. Congratulations!"

"Thanks, Dad."

But the surprises weren't over yet. With prot they never are. As everyone was leaving, he took me aside and whispered, "Karen has breast cancer. It's no problem now, but someone ought to take a look at it."

That night, when we had finally gotten to bed, I casually asked her when she was due for a mammogram.

"Funny you should ask about that. I just had one a month ago. It was negative. But prot suggested I make another appointment."

"Are you going to do it?"

"Right after the first of the year."

"Happy New Year," I said dismally.

"Don't be silly. This is what happens when you get old. Things start to go wrong. That's why we need to enjoy life now, before it's too late."

At that moment I promised myself I would definitely hang up my yellow pad as soon as possible after prot's imminent "departure."

I found out later that before he had showed up for Christmas he had somehow gotten into Ward Four and offered his genitalia for the taking by Charlotte. "I have no use for them," he apparently told her.

She merely laughed at him, explaining that she only took those from men who tried to hit on her. It was then that the whole sordid story of her own abuse by her *grandfather* came out. (As prot might have said, "People!") As of this writing she's engaged in intensive psychotherapy with Carl Thorstein, and he tells me there is some hope for a future for her after all!

It's events like this that make psychiatry and, for that matter, life on Earth, so thoroughly unpredictable.

SESSION FORTY-SEVEN

W HEN PROT came in for our final session, I had a basket of shiny apples ready for him.

"Red Delicious!" he exclaimed. "My favorite!"

"Yes," I murmured. "I know." After he had disposed of most of them, cores and all, I told him I wanted to say good-bye to Robert and the others.

He nodded and closed his eyes contentedly.

I waited for a moment. "How do you feel, Rob?"

No reply.

"Did you think about what we discussed last time?"

Probably, but he wasn't about to go through any further trauma on the eve of his departure for paradise, and who could blame him? All I could do was wish him godspeed. Maybe there was a slight response to that heartfelt sentiment, maybe not.

I watched him a few more minutes, wondering what he was thinking as he sat there frozen in time. Was he running in the field behind the house with his big dog, Apple? Gazing at the stars with his beloved father? Watching TV with his girlfriend Sarah? Tossing a giggling Gene into the air? Farewell, Rob. Farewell for now, my friend.

"Paul?"

He wasn't too eager to show up, either.

"Anything you want to get off your chest before you go?"

Apparently there wasn't.

I couldn't help thinking: He's going to be awfully disappointed by the women on K-PAX. "Good-bye, Paul, or whoever you are. And good luck to you."

He lifted his head for just a moment, winked, and replied, "I make my own luck."

"And Harry, you little devil. Take care of yourself and Rob."

Harry didn't make a move. He wasn't about to come out and get stuck with a needle.

"And don't get into any trouble!" I added like a worried father.

Though it doesn't show up clearly on the tape, I distinctly heard a muffled, "I won't!"

"Okay, prot, you can come on back now."

"Hello, hello, hello, hello," he spouted. One for each of them, I suppose.

"I just wanted to thank you again for all you've done for our patients."

"Not at all. I was well compensated for it." (He meant the fruit, presumably.)

"Prot, I've just got a few loose ends to tie up, okay?"

"If you say so. But there will always be more, no matter how many you tie up."

"No doubt. But I'd just like to clear up a few small matters before you go. For example, was Rob here last month? Or did he go to Guelph? Or somewhere else?"

"No idea, coach. You'll have to ask *him*."

It was far too late to point out that I *was* asking him. "Tell me this, then. Where did *you* go when you briefly left the hospital, now and two years ago?"

"To prepare those who would be going with me. And to offer my condolences to those who wouldn't."

"How did you know who wanted to go?"

He locked his hands behind his head and smiled, for all the world like someone who has accomplished some important task a little ahead of time. "The humans sent letters, remember? The others conveyed their wishes through the—uh—what you would probably call 'the grapevine.'"

"You mean the message is passed on from one being to the next—something like that?"

"Only far more complicated. When an elephant knows something, every elephant in the WORLD knows it."

"How can we verify that?"

"Ask them!"

"All right. Here's another question for you. You claim you age about seven months every time you come to Earth, right?"

"That's right!"

"So how could you travel halfway across the galaxy when Robin needed your help, and get there in time?" I asked smugly. "For that matter, why didn't it take seven months for his cry to get to K-PAX?"

"Gene, gene, gene. Haven't you heard anything I've said in the past 7.65 years? It takes no time at all to go from one place to another on the highest overtones of light energy. But time is relative for the traveler, and *he* ages a certain amount. Get it?"

"Not really." But there was little point in pursuing the matter. And it was time to say my final good-bye. "Any last words for me before you go, my alien friend?"

"Remember what I told you. You can solve the problems of any other being, and even a whole PLANET, if you could just learn to put yourself in his or her place. In fact, that's the *only* way you can do it."

"Thanks, I'll try to remember that."

Sensing there was nothing left for me to say, perhaps, he stood up.

"Just one last question."

"That'll be the day."

"Why only a hundred passengers? Why not two hundred? Or a thousand? Or a million?"

"I had no idea when I came here that damn near everybody wants to get off this WORLD. But next time . . ."

"Does that mean you've changed your mind and you'll be coming back?"

"Not a chance. But there might be others, and they'll know the score."

"How soon?"

He shrugged. "Maybe tomorrow. Maybe never. But if any other visitors do show up here, I hope you'll treat them well."

"Red Delicious and pitch-black bananas."

"Maybe my trip hasn't been for nothing after all!" He grabbed the remaining apples, stuffed them into a pocket, and, with a backward wave, was out the door.

"See you tomorrow," I murmured to myself as I stepped into my office, where Giselle was waiting with her son. She wanted him to say good-bye to me. Instead, he went for my nose.

"Thanks for everything you've done, Doctor B. Gene. And, if we don't see you again after tomorrow, don't worry about us. We'll be fine." She hugged me hard.

The only thing left to say was, "God bless us, every one."

That afternoon, prot, accompanied by most of the staff and patients, strode out to the front gate to say his final farewells to the huge crowd that had accumulated there. Someone had built a small platform next to the guardhouse and, despite the cold and snow, prot hopped onto it and stepped up to the microphone. There was an enthusiastic roar from the festive multitude, many of whom were waving "K-PAX" flags, which went on for several minutes. People were throwing gifts of fruit and flowers onto the little stage. Prot grinned broadly at them. (Someone told me later that it seemed he was speaking directly to every individual there, which included several dogs and cats, a few birds, and even a fish or two, held up high in their little bowls so he could see them.) Scattered here and there also were several vans and television cameras. Police were all over Amsterdam Avenue, which had been closed to traffic. I also spotted the G-men, unmistakable in their crew cuts and trim blue suits, up near the makeshift podium.

At last everything settled down and it became very quiet. "I'll be leaving you soon," he began, "and I shall miss you all."

Cries of "No!" were quickly stilled by an uplifted hand.

"Many of you understand that a great many changes need to be made to turn your beautiful EARTH into the paradise it could be. I have said consistently that how you do this is something you have to work out for yourselves. Yet I keep getting cards and letters telling me you don't know where to begin. Nothing could be simpler. *First, do no harm, either to your PLANET or any of your fellow beings—*"

Suddenly a shot rang out. At exactly that instant prot tilted his head to the side and the bullet whizzed past him, piercing his left ear. A scuffle broke out in the crowd and several people grappled with the gunman. Someone took the weapon away, and another man grabbed the woman's arm and twisted it around her back. She screamed, and there was a lot of other noise and confusion.

Prot, the blood running down his cheek, lifted his hand again and said, without raising his voice in the slightest, "Leave her alone. She's just following orders she received years ago from her family, her friends, and almost everyone else she knows. Don't hurt her, don't throw her in jail. Teach her."

By now, Chak had climbed onto the podium and clamped a gauze onto prot's damaged ear. He went on as if nothing had happened. "And now, my friends, I must leave you. Some day, if you somehow survive the twenty-first century, other K-PAXians may visit you. And who knows—some of your grandchildren may make the trip to the other side of the GALAXY. It's not so far away, really." He waved again, jumped down from the platform, Chak trailing along behind, and trotted back inside.

Long after the commotion had died down, the crowd finally began to disperse, except for a few souvenir hunters who lingered. In an hour or two the sidewalk was clear, and cars and taxis were once again honking past the gate. It was as if prot had never been here.

That evening there was another huge party in the Ward Two lounge, organized by my wife and Betty McAllister. Everyone was there, including most of the former patients who had departed the hospital in the past seven and a half years: Howie, Ernie, Chuck and Mrs. Archer, Maria in her nun's habit, Ed and LaBelle Chatte, Whacky and his voluptuous girlfriend, Lou and her daughter Protista, Rudolph, Michael and his new wife, Jackie and her stepfather, Bert, and all the others who had come into contact with prot. Some of my own family were there, too, including Abby and Steve and the boys, Freddy and two of his lady friends, and Will and Dawn, who was beginning to look something like the *Mona Lisa*. Cassandra was already predicting that the unborn child, a boy, would grow up to be a psychiatrist! I told her we would see about that.

Frankie, the lucky winner of an all-expenses-paid trip to Utopia, was all smiles (though she affectionately called everyone she ran into an "anal orifice") as were Giselle and little Gene. They were all so happy, in fact, that I almost wished I were going with them. I knew, of course, that tomorrow morning the sky was going to fall and I would have to deal not only with their devastating disappointment, but with that of Robert Porter as well.

Even so, I didn't want to spoil the party, and it was well past midnight when it finally broke up and all the patients made their tearful farewells and went to their beds. I finally escorted prot, along with Giselle and her son, to his room, where they would all spend the night, or what was left of it. "Well, thanks again," I murmured, taking his hand.

"Enjoy your retirement, gino," he responded. "You've earned it."

Giselle thrust the baby into his arms and gave me another hug and a kiss, smack on the mouth. Prot, with no experience in such matters, held him as though he were the most fragile thing in the universe.

I took my godson from him and kissed him on the forehead. "Good-bye, kid," I told him, tweaking his little nose. "Don't take any wooden yorts."

"My beings didn't raise no dummies," I distinctly heard him reply, unless prot was an expert ventriloquist along with everything else.

I was up early the next morning with Chak and the rest of the medical staff, trying to prepare for anything that might happen. I was especially concerned about a possible storm of mass hysteria, which would have been a nightmare. "Not to worry at all," he kept telling me. "Everything will be very fine."

We got to the dining room before seven, but prot and his "family" were already there, gorging themselves on cereal (with rice milk) and fruit. It was a quiet breakfast, most of the patients having decided to let them enjoy their last meal on Earth in private.

Prot, wearing his usual blue corduroys and denim shirt, seemed his normal self—unconcerned, confident. He lapped up at least a quart of orange juice, several dishes of prunes, and one last bunch of overripe bananas. I noticed that his ear was still bandaged. K-PAXians, it appeared, were as slow to heal as the rest of us.

"Well, it's time," he said, when all the fruit was gone except for the dried ones, which he was taking with him.

There was a last piney hug from Giselle, and even a quick one from Frankie. "Get that nose fixed," she admonished. Prot thanked me for "your patience" (patients?), and hoped that "all your mental problems will be little ones."

A few of the inmates and staff said their final farewells and wandered over to the lounge, where many of the others had already assembled, as had the CIA, with their sensors, recorders, and cameras. The press photographers waited impatiently on the other side of the room. Apparently there was little time left. Prot immediately gathered the three of them together, brought out his little mirror and flashlight, and gave one last wave (each of us was sure he was waving to him or her). Frankie, blowing kisses, shouted, "Good-bye, you bastards! Fuck you all! Fuck you . . . ! Fuck you . . . !"

I yelled at prot, "Say hello to Bess for me!" He winked, but whether this meant "I will" or he was complimenting me on my sense of humor, I'll never know. In any case he clearly mouthed, "Don't eat anyone I know!", held out his little mirror, propped the flashlight on his shoulder, switched it on, and in an instant he was gone.

I didn't know what Giselle and the others' reaction would be when it was over, but I expected Robert to collapse on the spot where prot had stood, as he had done the last time prot departed. Instead, he disappeared too, as did Frankie, Giselle, and the boy. All of them had simply vanished.

A few minutes later I got a call from my wife. "Oxie is gone," she chirped, without the slightest hint of disappointment.

Somehow I wasn't surprised.

Epilogue

SHORTLY AFTER prot and the others had "disappeared," there was a call from the Bronx zoo. Several of the primates had somehow gotten out and hadn't been found. To this day none of them has turned up anywhere, but whether they accompanied prot on his final "journey" to K-PAX, no one knows.

But this we do know: About a dozen humans from around the world were also reported missing shortly after our group of five (counting Oxeye) departed. Many of these declared, on the morning of December 31, that they were waiting for someone to pick them up. Some even left notes giving a forwarding address: K-PAX. The only former patients who disappeared at about the same time as the others were Ed (and his cat LaBelle)—prot, apparently, had fulfilled a long-standing promise to them—and Mr. Magoo, the man who couldn't recognize faces, which would be of little consequence on K-PAX.

So far as we can determine, however, none of the children who wanted to go with prot were chosen. Indeed, there have been several reports that prot visited some of the juvenile applicants at one time or another over the past two years to explain why he wouldn't be taking them with him. In every case he told them the same thing he had told all the young people hanging around the gate for the past month: They could have K-PAX right here if they wanted it badly enough, it was up to them, etc.

As for the seventy or so remaining "seats," we can only guess that they were filled by various beings from giraffes to bugs. The only thing we can be fairly certain about is that there were probably no sea creatures included in the passenger list.

So where are prot and all the others? Maybe they're hiding out in some cave in Antarctica or under the canopy of a dense South American jungle. Or perhaps they are all on K-PAX. Wherever they went, they disappeared without a trace and haven't been seen since, except for a number of reports of his abducting a few more rural Midwest couples for sexual purposes, and flying over large cities like some latter-day Superman. Prot, of course, would have dismissed these as "background noise."

It all boils down to this: There are two possible explanations for what happened to them, equally plausible in my view. The first is that prot was no more and no less than a secondary personality of a deeply disturbed young man devastated by the terrible events of his boyhood. Like certain autists he was somehow able to reach into recesses of his brain that the rest of us, for whatever reasons, can't get to. This would account for his ability to trick us into believing he could travel faster than light, come up with complex cosmological theories, and so on.

Moreover, he somehow managed to change not only the spectral acuity of his eyesight but the structure of the DNA within the very cells of his body. (Only prot's DNA differed from Robert's. That of Paul and Harry did not.) He may also have been able to read minds, though there isn't much clear evidence for that. And certainly bodies, thank God. He correctly diagnosed not only former patient Russell's bowel tumor in 1990, but my wife's breast cancer seven years later. (Karen had a tiny malignancy removed early in 1998 and the prognosis is excellent.) Not to mention all the psychiatric patients he set on the road to recovery with his uncanny intuition. The little boxes he gave us all for Christmas, incidentally, turned out to be infinite regressions. No matter how powerful the microscope, there was always another box inside.

The only other possible explanation is that prot can see UV light and travel at tachyon speeds, and that he is on K-PAX right now introducing a hundred of our fellow beings to his Garden of Eden in the sky. Fantastic, yes, but little more so than the former hypothesis, I have come to believe.

Let's examine the latter explanation for a moment. Does it fit the data? How can we account for the fact that prot and Robert seemed to occupy the same body, at least at times? Is it possible that only prot's spirit or essence came to Earth, something that he himself denied? More to the point, if only the essences of the hundred space travelers left the planet, where are their bodies? Alternatively, did prot's entire being make the trip to Earth and, for reasons beyond our understanding, could somehow replace Robert at a moment's notice? But if he really was a space traveler, how do we account for the apparent similarities in the lives of prot on his ideal planet and Robert here on Earth?

I have thought about these possibilities long and hard, believe me, and the only conclusion I have been able to reach is that the truth is "all of the above." Or to put it another way, the answer is a combination of both explanations. Isn't it possible, for instance, that planet K-PAX is a kind of alternate world to our own, a parallel universe, so to speak, one of the roads not taken on Earth? Do we all have alter egos floating somewhere among the stars?

Whatever the answer, there are a great many questions still lying in the folder labeled "Robert Porter." For example, how did Rob manage to fool us in 1995 with his apparent "pseudorecovery," and who else was in on the deception? And was it Harry who did away with the intruder who murdered Rob's wife and daughter, and what would have happened if that vicious killer hadn't appeared that fateful day in August, 1985—would Robert and his family have lived a relatively normal life? What if six-year-old Rob had never bathed his father? Or little Gene? Or if his father had never been injured in the first place? Or Giselle had wheels? Will prot and the others ever return? Wherever they are, have they found, at last, a measure of the peace they all so desperately sought?

In brief, I don't know the answers to any of these questions. All I know is that I have hung up my yellow pad and moved to an old farmhouse in the Adirondacks (courtesy of the film version of *K-PAX*), where Karen and I, and our mixed-breed dog Flower, plan to sit and watch the sun go down till the end of our days. I leave the world in the hands of the next generations, who, I dearly hope, and choose to believe, are up to the job.

In one case, at least, I have absolute faith in the future. My son Will, now doing his residency at Bellevue, is going to be a fine psychiatrist, of that I am certain. He has an ability I never had, that of empathizing with his patients and getting things out of them that no one else can. He claims he learned this trick from prot, but I think it was something he was born with. He and Dawn are now the parents of a beautiful baby boy who resembles his grandfather in many ways (you should compare our baby pictures!), and they come up to see us whenever they get a chance, though Will claims that taking care of the old house, in addition to his professional duties, takes most of his time.

Freddy visits less often, usually for a brief "weekend" (following his Sunday matinée). Now living with a new soulmate in the West Village (the real thing this time, he tells us), he is still a regular cast member of the popular Broadway show *Les Misérables*.

With prot's help, our son-in-law Steve is now chair of the astronomy department at Princeton. Consequently, he has little time for research or anything else, including us (his predecessor, Charlie Flynn, incidentally, is now a student at a Midwestern theology school). But his and Abby's kids, now approaching adulthood (too soon!), are our most frequent visitors, especially in the summer, when they usually stay for several weeks, claiming they don't miss their computers a bit. Abby herself survived turning forty, and is more active than ever in various "rights" causes.

Jennifer, the "real doctor" in the family, doesn't visit us as much as we'd like (though we have been to see *her* once or twice), but she keeps us informed on the progress of her AIDS practice and research. She tells us, in fact, that she is participating in a program to test a new vaccine against HIV and it looks as though it is going to be a godsend.

Do I miss the grind? Not much. Retirement is every bit as good as it's supposed to be. I do keep up with some of the psychiatric literature and visit the hospital once in a while, where Jerry and I usually have a heart-to-heart, his head against my chest, or vice versa. And I have met the woman who took the pot-shot at prot, now a patient at MPI. She claims she was acting "under orders from God." Whenever I see her I remember prot's telling me that wherever there are religions there will always be fanatics.

Thorstein is still there, as are Goldfarb and all the rest; they were kind enough to rename the lecture hall between the first and second floors the "E.N. Brewer Auditorium" (the new wing is still under construction), probably hoping for a large donation from me. Although that expectation hasn't yet been realized, I am nevertheless deeply grateful for the honor.

But I'm beginning to feel like an outsider there, especially since most of the old, pre-prot patients are gone. Just as well. Let Will be the next Brewer beating his brains against the prots and Christs and the other unfortunate people who end up within those walls.

Not that we aren't keeping busy (I still haven't found time to read *Moby Dick*, or try the unicycle Milton presented to me on the eve of his departure). Karen is firmly in charge of our travel schedule and all our social and cultural engagements, including an occasional performance at the Met, and keeps us pretty busy. But now I see opera (and a number of other things) in a rather different light since prot's visits. It is, after all, limited to the joys and tragedies of people. If there's one thing I learned from him, it's that we humans seem to be concerned with only a tiny part of some larger whole. According to prot, every being has just as much right to its life as we do, a view I have finally come to share, though I still have a slice of pizza or a hot fudge sundae once in a while. But no more cottage cheese!

And I spend more time now looking at the sky. In fact, Karen bought me a four-inch reflecting telescope for my retirement present, and most clear evenings, summer and winter, will find me outside contemplating the stars. Sometimes I look toward the constellation Lyra and wonder whether our hundred beings are up there and what they are doing (part of me will always regret not accepting prot's offer of a free trip to K-PAX when I had the chance). I sincerely hope they have found peace and contentment, and that there is another world out there where my father is still alive and I became a singer instead of a psychiatrist. Whether that is true or only a dream, there's one thing I'm absolutely sure of: There are millions of planets we don't yet know about, worlds we can hope to visit or communicate with some day, and the Earth and the beings on it aren't at the center of the universe. Rather, I see us, the galaxy, and even the universe itself as a tiny part of the wisdom, beauty, and mystery of God.

Suggested Additional Reading

Abbey, Lloyd, *The Last Whales* (Grove Weidenfeld, New York, 1989).

Amory, Cleveland, *Mankind?* (Harper and Row, New York, 1974).

Bliss, E.L., *Multiple Personality, Allied Disorders, and Hypnosis* (Oxford Press, New York and Oxford, 1986).

Brewer, Gene, *K-PAX* (St. Martin's Press, New York, 1995).

Brewer, Gene, *On a Beam of Light* (St. Martin's Press, New York, 2001).

Buell, R., and Zimmer, N., *Aspects of Love: The Doctor/Patient Relationship* (Cityscape Press, Buffalo, NY, 1991).

Calder, Nigel, *Einstein's Universe* (Viking Press, New York, 1979).

Carson, Rachel, *Silent Spring* (Houghton Mifflin, Boston, 1962).

Cavalieri, Paola, and Singer, Peter, *The Great Ape Project* (St. Martin's Press, New York, 1993).

Confer, W.N., and Ables, B.S., *Multiple Personality* (Human Sciences Press, Inc., New York, 1983).

Croswell, Ken, *The Universe at Midnight* (The Free Prees, New York, 2001).

Davison, Gerald C., and Neale, John M., *Abnormal Psychology* (John Wiley & Sons, New York, 1994).

Dressler, Alan, *Voyage to the Great Attractor* (Alfred A. Knopf, New York, 1994).

Ehrlich, Paul, *The Population Bomb* (Ballantine Books, New York, 1968).

Eisenberg, Evan, *The Ecology of Eden* (Alfred A. Knopf, New York, 1998).

Ferris, Timothy, *The Whole Shebang* (Simon & Schuster, New York, 1997).

Friedman, C.T.H., and Gaguet, R.A. (eds.), *Extraordinary Disorders of Human Behavior* (Plenum Press, New York, 1982).

Garrett, Laura, *The Coming Plague* (Farrar, Straus and Giroux, New York, 1994).

Griffin, Giselle, *An Alien among Us?* (Scientific Publications, Inc., Montpelier, VT, 1996).

Havens, L., *A Safe Place* (Harvard University Press, Cambridge, MA, 1989).

Hawking, Stephen, *A Brief History of Time* (Bantam Books, New York, 1988).

Jamison, K.R., *Touched With Fire* (The Free Press, New York, 1992).

Mason, Jim, *An Unnatural Order* (Simon & Schuster, New York, 1993).

Masson, Jeffrey M., & McCarthy, S., *When Elephants Weep* (Delacorte Press, New York, 1995).

McKibben, Bill, *The End of Nature* (Random House, New York, 1989).

Melville, Herman, *Moby Dick* (Harper & Bros., New York, 1851).

Neale, J.M. *et al.*, *Case Studies of Abnormal Psychology* (J. Wiley, New York, 1982).

Payne, K., *Silent Thunder* (Simon & Schuster, New York, 1998).

prot, *Preliminary Observations on B-TIK* (RX 4987165.233), unpublished.

Putnam, F., *Diagnosis and Treatment of Multiple Personality Disorder* (Guildford Press, New York, 1989).

Quammen, David, *The Song of the Dodo* (Simon & Schuster, New York, 1996).

Rapoport, J.L., The *Boy Who Couldn't Stop Washing* (E. P. Dutton, New York, 1989).

Restak, R.M., *The Mind* (Bantam Books, New York, 1988).

Robbins, J., *Diet for a New America* (Stillpoint Publications, Walpole, NH, 1987).

Sacks, Oliver, *The Man Who Mistook His Wife for a Hat* (HarperCollins Publishers, New York, 1985).

Sacks, Oliver, *An Anthropologist on Mars* (Alfred A. Knopf, New York, 1995).

Sagan, Carl, *The Dragons of Eden* (Random House, New York, 1977).

Sagan, Carl, *Cosmos* (Random House, New York, 1980).

Sagan, Carl, *The Demon-Haunted World* (Random House, New York, 1995).

Schell, Jonathan, *The Fate of the Earth* (Alfred A. Knopf, New York, 1982).

Singer, P., *Animal Liberation* (Avon Books, New York, 1975).

Sizemore, C.C., A *Mind of My Own* (W. Morrow, New York, 1989).

Stone, I., *The Passions of the Mind* (Doubleday, New York, 1971).

Taylor, Gordon R., *The Biological Time Bomb* (New American Library, Cleveland, 1968).

Treen, A., and Treen, S., *The Dalmatian* (Howell Book House, New York, 1980).

Treffert, D.A., *Extraordinary People* (Harper & Row, New York, 1989).

Wise, S., *Rattling the Cage* (Perseus Books, Cambridge, MA, 2000).

Wolman, B. (ed.), *The Therapist's Handbook* (van Nostrand Reinhold, New York, 1983).

Yalom, Irvin D., *Love's Executioner* (Basic Books, New York, 1989).

ACKNOWLEDGMENTS

I thank Lois Weinstein for climbing this mountain with me. Also my editors Mike Jones and Elizabeth O'Malley for their interest and generosity, and Sarah-Jane Forder for outstanding copyediting.

A NOTE ON THE AUTHOR

Before becoming a novelist, Gene Brewer studied DNA
replication and cell division at several major research
institutions. He lives in New York City and is the author of
K-PAX and *K-PAX II: On a Beam of Light*. *K-PAX III:
The Worlds of Prot* is the third and final part of the K-PAX
trilogy.